Potomac Review

Potomac Review

EDITOR
John Wei Han Wang

POETRY EDITOR
Katherine Smith

NONFICTION EDITOR
Albert Kapikian

COVER DESIGN
Lotte Marie Allen

ADMINISTRATIVE ASSISTANT/WEBMASTER
Om B. Rusten

ASSOCIATE EDITORS

Dianne Bosser
Collin Brown
Kenneth Fleming
Courtney Ford
Robert Giron
Michael Landweber
Michael LeBlanc
Kateema Lee

David Lott
Mike Maggio
David Saitzeff
Jessie Seigel
Marianne Szlyk
Karolina Wilk
Sherri Woosley
Hananah Zaheer

INTERNS
Spencer Adkins
Yemaya Alleyne
Vida Branco
Victoria Sookoo

Potomac Review is a journal of fiction, poetry, and nonfiction
published by the Paul Peck Humanities Institute at
Montgomery College, Rockville
51 Mannakee Street, Rockville, MD 20850

Potomac Review has been made possible through
the generosity of Montgomery College.

A special thanks to Dean Rodney Redmond.

For submission guidelines and more information:
www.potomacreview.org

Potomac Review, Inc. is a not-for-profit 501 c(3) corp.
Member, Council of Literary Magazines & Presses
Indexed by the American Humanities Index
ISBN: 978-0-9990403-1-7
ISSN: 1073-1989

SUBSCRIBE TO POTOMAC REVIEW
One year at $24 (2 issues)
Two years at $36 (4 issues)
Sample copy order, $10 (single issue)

TABLE OF CONTENTS

Nonfiction

MAGNOLIA

1.

Magnolia was born twelve weeks too soon, on a rainy Saturday in October. That morning, ten-year-old Cedric put the kettle on the stove and sat at the kitchen table in the blue predawn, listening to the thunder. In the courtyard of The Galaxie Apartments, the dead leaves made sounds like applause. The kettle whistled, and Cedric heard his grandmother get up. Cedric thinks his grandmother is magnificent, even though she had to quit her job at the pharmacy, even though now she makes mops at Industries for the Blind. As he heated milk for the oatmeal, Cedric knew she was sitting barefoot at her dressing table in her pink terrycloth robe, powdering her face in the dark, braiding her thick white hair with long, elegant fingers. Since she lost her vision there is something fiercer about her, and when she disciplines him, he imagines he's being held captive by a blind queen.

After breakfast, Cedric asked his grandmother if she wanted to go with him to the rehab facility. She shook her head, and Cedric left her like he did every Saturday, sitting in the recliner, drinking peppermint tea and listening to smooth jazz on the radio. She used to tell Cedric stories of his mother Before. His mother in the kitchen in the house Cedric couldn't remember, making shrimp gumbo or sausage jambalaya. His mother listening to her favorite Christmas album in July,

1

singing "Baby, It's Cold Outside" while dancing Cedric around the living room. But his grandmother told these stories less often with each of his mother's stints away from home—in jail, or court-mandated rehab, or the hospital—and for the past three months, Cedric has ridden the bus downtown alone.

2.

She had no official name, only an identification number, Fetus Girl #2567. When Cedric asked the nurse what would happen to her, she told him that someone from the Medical Examiner's Office would pick up the body, which would be buried in the Cemetery for the Unclaimed. Cedric hesitated, then told the nurse that he would very much like to hold it. The nurse looked at his mother, who shrugged and closed her eyes. The nurse placed the small, swaddled thing in Cedric's hands.

Cedric named her Magnolia because her skin was soft and rubbery and reminded him of the thick white petals that fell from the tree in the front yard of the Galaxie. She was nearly as light as a balloon in his arms. She was smaller than a loaf of bread but bigger than the kitten he'd held at Brandon's house. Her fists were the size of gumballs. Cedric stared for a long time into her crushed, indignant face. He was filled with a deep desire for her to know things: that the cartons of chocolate milk in the school cafeteria tasted like cardboard and that this made it better, somehow, than chocolate milk in a glass. Or that you feel homesick when you realize you are too old for things, like Santa Claus or the playground at McDonald's or balloon animals. He wanted to make her a toasted cheese sandwich. He wanted to sing her his favorite country song.

The nurse left the room to *give them a minute*. Cedric's mother rolled over to face the wall. Cedric pressed the still, small creature against his cheek and watched his mother move under the sheets. The longer he watched, the more alien she became, until her movements seemed not to belong to a person at all. Cedric knelt on the floor, balancing the baby on his lap. He emptied his backpack and placed Magnolia inside. His mother still had her back to him as he zipped up the bag and walked quickly from the room. It wasn't until he reached the bus stop that Cedric realized he'd left his math book behind.

Cedric waited for the bus in the rain. While he waited, he considered the consequences of his actions. He understood the consequences for losing his math book: his grandmother would be very disappointed, because textbooks were expensive, and he should know better. Mrs. Harris would make him look on for the rest of the year with his neighbor, who was Nathan, who was mean, who always had purple lips from the grape popsicle he ate at lunch. Cedric was less certain of the consequences for claiming his sister. He tightened his grip on the backpack as the rain soaked through his sneakers. He hoped it hadn't hurt. He hoped Magnolia's soul had taken to the sky like a kite on a beach in winter, her faded papery soul drifting on ribbons of air.

3.

When Cedric gets home, the blind queen is away from the castle. After trying to find a place for her (shoebox, pajama drawer, Lego fort) Cedric decides to keep Magnolia in a fishbowl on the windowsill of his bedroom. The fishbowl had previously belonged to Lucky, who had been a good fish, who had lived three years and four months, well past the life expectancy of Lucky's type of fish, which was Black Molly, which Cedric knew to be twelve to eighteen months from a book on fish he'd checked out of the library. Also, Lucky was a carnival fish. Cedric won him at the school fair. His mother had warned him that carnival fish don't ever live very long and told him not to get too attached.

Cedric fears that becoming too attached might be one of the consequences of claiming Magnolia. He wraps a small, ticking clock in a dishtowel and places it next to the bowl, just as Brandon's mother had done when they got their new puppy. She'd explained that it would remind the puppy of his mother's heartbeat and help him be less homesick. Cedric doesn't want Magnolia to be homesick. He tries to remember being unborn. He tries to remember whether his mother's heartbeat had sounded anything like a ticking clock wrapped in a dishtowel.

FATHER FIGURE

he says, *i've got a daughter*
your age. the moon is six times
too big, glowing orange as a luminescent
pumpkin, growing over the street lamps,
and the sidewalk, and me. i've been counting every
time he takes a drag per minute.
i imagine his eyes as hers, little blue
marbles, same shade as the ocean
of my little blue globe eraser i lost
in the third grade. she could have been
in my class (she wasn't, but she could
have been). i am close to
drunk, smacking my lips after every
gulp of the tequila sunrise that is much more
tequila than sunrise. *i don't usually*
do this, his lips say, but his eyes, with their blue
orbs — they say something different. they say, *i know how*
this ends, i've been here before. they say, *i haven't*
seen my daughter in three months, and i don't
care. i say, *okay,* and we end
in his bed, lights out and clothes
abandoned.   but i can't quite forget her.

THE LUNCH

I am bringing him lunch on 89th Street
and we are going to sing.
While he waits, he'll read the paper
and turn his radios on in two rooms.
I want to plan the meal right:
Rolls with butter, eclairs and chocolate leaves,
swordfish and potato chips and Mallomars,
bagels and fruit cup, nonpareils, a cake.
I start again with rolls and butter, wrapping them in gold.

But then I think we'll meet instead on Edgewood Avenue
where on Saturdays he spread the news
around the dining room and we cleaned the cage,
filled the seed cups and the hanging water trough,
and the canary he chose for its beautiful voice, flew, amazed,
before my father set it back, gently, on its perch,
and went upstairs, startled cat in tow,
to his white desk to write.

Or is it better to eat together at the long table
in the L-shaped house on Windmill Lane,
with its narrow cathedral window in the high fireplace of stone,
a Japanese maple and dark Asian shrubs, and empty fish ponds,
where he laughed in the alcove, typing fast.

Or if I keep walking straight and north,
under the deep green awning and down a hall,
I can unpack our lunch on the woven mats
where we ate before and he put the records on,
and I felt too shy to join him as he sang "Old Devil Moon."
So I will sing it with him now.

I have my basket and platters, full and ready, to set down,
but at which house, what table,
when all the locks are changed?
If I go where my father is,
I have to ask someone to show the way
to the section, his row, a tree.
I need a map to find him.
And how will I carry all these things with my pockets full of
    stones?

A FRIEND OF THE ZOO

Errol Condon's office is not a bright affair. Lead animal sculptures barely restrain his paper stacks and the ceiling freaks out in a swoop of parrot mobiles. Old pinups of Giant Pandas — pandas who no longer exist or have been repatriated to Sichuan — festoon his wall panels. There is Frank the Wildebeest, and Lonnie, the lion curator who died of angina pectoris, there giving a thumbs-up in his safari tans under the pre-renovation Monorail. There's one of Jamie Marquez, who managed the sea lion sanctuary. Jamie is a married woman — and who'd of believed it, Errol thinks. Bo Hendricks smiles and he ran the elephants. Now he's 6 by 8 and lives above a cheeping radiator as an immortalized raker of dung. A lot of vivid snapshots of a Bronx past contained — Italians, the borough prez chummy in a porkpie handshaking some natty union guys, Graig Nettles in a batting stance from '77 when the Pinstripes took the Bronx back from the Son of Sam. Condon is Bronx-bred, harrowed by memories. One can find him on Arthur Avenue, teasing caramel ambrosia from his marron glacé, wishing the neighborhood young again.

Errol Condon leaves his office and knows he will snoop on one of his volunteer docents.

There is a line forming, contouring to the triple-pane glass which separates the great apes in their crouches from the viewing hordes. Edith Frankel is looming. She wears a logo identifier like a laminated pendulum around her neck — "Volunteer Docent'" below that, the typical grinning passport shot — and a statement of who she is underneath it.

The gorillas are grooming each other, and it is a heartening sight, their quarried rocks a nice spot to animate some primeval theatrics, and the standing crowd melts, the general thinking being, "They are just like us, but nicer." Something about their motions suggest robots in a slow reckoning that, contrary to their wiring, they can now feel. There are a lot of peering children in today. Edith is always there for questions. Eight decades, jaw dewlaps, and edematous wrists and ankles don't stop her. She stalks up on a viewing huddle.

"Do you have a question for me?" she says.

"How long do the gorillas live?" asks a winsome little boy.

"Now with these gorillas, maybe to fifty or sixty," says Edith. "With the breeds in Africa and the rainforests, about half that. We take care of them here, clean their teeth, scrub their gums, groom them for tick-borne diseases. When they're in for that kind of top treatment, they last."

"So when they lose their teeth they —"

"They can't eat, that's right. They starve."

The boy's father interjects, "You would think evolution would provide for longer life. I mean if they can be kept alive by simple teeth-cleaning you would think Nature would find a way to have them do it."

"Nature doesn't ask anything of us but that we fuck," says Edith. "So we can, you know, reproduce the organisms. Once these hairy females reach menopause, they're good for pretty much nothing."

She taps the glass and makes a neck-slitting motion at the ape. The crowd is in mild-gasp, but the child ventures forward.

"What is menopause?"

"When a woman can't have any more babies," answers Edith.

"But when does it happen?"

"Often around forty."

"My mother is forty-one," says the child.

"Yeah, well. You can pretty much throw her off the fire escape at this point."

The child clubs his own face with his mitten.

"Come on, sweetie, she's just a crazy old woman," his father says, shuttling him away.

Edith moves further down the viewing glass, where stylish Brazilians look on.

"God, they have so much coarse fur," says a woman.

"Not so much," says Edith. "You ever see a hairy Jew on the beach? Makes these things look like Yul Brynner. Now Marvin Rifkind spent a month of Sundays going through my Norman's estate, had me down in Pompano to go through the assets. We took a day just laying out and reading *The Winds of War*, and I almost cried, but that's another story. But this man's chest—you could disappear in it like some poor fuck in Vietnam."

"Miss," says a stunning Brazilian with a wild black mane. "Where are the Emperor Tamarins? The little monkeys, my son wants to see them."

"*Do I look like I know from Tamarins?*" screams Edith. "Go back to Ipanema and shave your box!"

The Brazilians clear out in an oxygen vacuum.

Go, Edith, go, whispers Errol. Don't let them out. Take it to the Bastille.

Edith sidles up to a family from Detroit. "Do you know gorillas learn?" she says. "I was no good at math but I was a special ace at literature. I went to Hunter College for one year with my friend Bernice."

"That so," says the father, looking straight ahead at the animals.

"Bernice got around, very popular. Now that Judy Symcowitz—a railroader of a *lot* of men, a real pump—used to rope me into Mah Jong and wouldn't you know it, those gossipers, those unconscionable yentas in Crotona Park, were always chewing on this notion I was this slut! Well let me tell *you* something! I was not. Bernice Krumholtz is the one. Oh she was so glamorous; yeah, spent a weekend with some cousin of Henry Cabot Lodge, yeah. But she settled. I'll tell you, that Neapolitan peasant that she married never had a hard-on she didn't coddle. She babied that fucking thing like it had colic!"

Heads swivel. A stroller is motored away like an ambulance. A mother holding a young one in a papoose skips off.

Just entered, a family of Bainbridge Avenue Irish stare warmly at the mandrills on display. A marmoset teases fate and ambles down a sprouted copse to a where a silverback knuckles on bowlegs towards the family, thinking their paleness strange: there are no soccer jerseys in the western lowlands. The gorilla delivers a Congo snuffle. Edith hears the brogues, the clover chuckles, and insinuates herself near the clan.

"Do you have any questions for me?"

A large silverback rubbing his breastbone sensually in front of them bears his gums to the Irishman's sheer delight.

"Yes," he answers, a cuddly pad of red hair atop his face as wide as a pumpkin. "Such expressions. How do they do it?"

"It's the sagittal crest," says Edith. "Runs like a black fin over the skull and powers the facial muscles."

"Really?"

"They have to chew a lot of tough meats. I never used a tenderizer. My husband hated my meat, and I didn't like his either!"

"Ah," says the Irishman, confused.

The Dutchman returns his gaze to the ape.

"I hear they have the ability of knowledge," he says.

"Yes, some do," says Edith. "The Koko makes family bonds. Even signs and can imagine a past and future. They like to look at each other when they screw."

"Hmm," he says. He looks at the nametag, bewildered. "You uh, you *work* here?"

"You know these are the *real* urban gorillas here," says Edith, suddenly turning to a platinum-headed Dutchwoman in back of the Irishman.

"Yes," says the woman.

"I don't know why they call them 'Urban Gorillas,'" says Edith with honest consternation. "I mean they called that Patty Hearst one, and she was no gorilla. She was an attractive woman! Not quite a beauty, I'll say, but you know, you know, attractive. And with that gun, you know, the picture with that Tommy gun she was modeling up against the cobra flag, she was even *more* attractive!"

"I think the spelling is g-u-e-r-r-i-l-l-a, Miss," interjects a smiling Dutchman wearing wraparound, orange-tinted specs. "It is a Spanish word. It is a fighter."

"Well, whatever it is, she was more attractive with the gun than without. You fuck."

"I beg your pardon?"

"What are you, swimming the freestyle? You look like a walleye in those things!"

"Yes. Why are you harassing him?" says an old woman, her accent strikingly London toff.

"Hey," says Edith to the woman, all of a sudden reverting to a schoolgirl. "You sound like the PBS people who narrate those *Masterpiece* shows. The ones where the whole house sips tea and a horseman strips some married dingbat down to her garters and fucks her into Pluto on a four-poster while the husband with the mustache plans World War One."

"You don't say."

Edith shrugs. Errol bites happily into an apple. The Congo chamber, a multi-buffer zone of rug and glass, feels hushed and bustling simultaneously. The silverback pounds its chest. Its brother, a yard above on the maximally landscaped copse, models a pink erection, presenting it as a stemmed tulip to an Ecuadorian girl, who cowers behind her father.

Edith says to the tiny man concealing his daughter, "Milton Berle was supposed to have a huge cock he liked to show to people when they were dressing in their changing rooms. Now *that* was scary."

The Ecuadorian, uncomprehending, grunts.

"He was a very funny man," says Edith. She bends and pinches the little girl's cheek and picks at the ribbon in her hair, straightening it. Errol smiles, lets his abdomen stick out. Roar, baby, he whispers, roar.

Another morning in the hopper. Errol goes back to his office. He answers twenty-two email complaints, assuring the insulted he will address the situation comprehensively. He drinks his instant coffee and lets the heat of the brew tickle the coils of his throat. He is enjoying this gig for the first time in ages, at least since Sharfstein began his tenure.

Errol has been a zoo man twenty-five years and has shepherded the volunteer program for all the zoo's primate displays — Jungleworld, Madagascar, the Congo Gorilla Forest with its legions of tailless gibbons in perpetual knuckle-drag, and, of course, the Baboon Reserve. The program is neither boondoggle nor moneybags but it is near to a lasting source of pride. He has seventy-one Friends of the Zoo trained as unpaid docents. He has remedial science kids from DeWitt Clinton High and even some Rikers Island recidivists working off guide sheets at the lar gibbon groves. The docents have a way of ticking off the veteran curators, whose empathy often ends at the animal pens. They don't sit too well with Sharfstein either, who is a stickler for streamlining things. Errol persists. It is hard to wake up with nothing but a sandwich to live for, he tells the curators; it is hard to block out the tinnitus that might chime from the nearing death knell. Were someone like Edith not here, she might find herself pastured with the lolling cadavers at a rest home, tottering openmouthed while a maniacally jovial volunteer plinked "High Hopes" on a freestanding synth. That is how it often ends; humans don't get euthanized without committing animal crimes.

He sips his coffee and sets to work. To a complainant from Mississauga, Ontario, he replies:

Dear Ms. Conifer,

I hope this letter finds you well. I was terribly troubled to hear your son was told that Wayne Gretzky "tossed a mean salad." We will rectify the situation and terminate that volunteer docent. Our vetting process cannot always account for surges in infarct dementia, or whatever neurocranial adversity might have precipitated the regrettable outburst. (It might just be what she's like?) Rest assured, we are committed to making your zoo visit a happy and unmolested experience. I trust you will understand that this incident is the exception, not the rule, and that the problem has been handled expeditiously.

Sincerely,

Errol Condon

Director of Volunteer Docents

He will not fire Edith, of course. He will give her more hours. He will make her a mainstay of the apes. It's only a matter of keeping it all in-house. Eric Sharfstein must not know, but he must pay. He must suffer. His operation must be subverted.

Errol would have lived a full and happy life not knowing Eric Sharfstein was a person; Sharfstein who somehow leapfrogged him in the space of no time to become Director of Primate Attractions; Sharfstein with his face of a hack sportscaster, his risible non-zoo creds. It does not escape Errol that, before his tenure here, Sharfstein sold lithium batteries out of a suitcase in Hempstead, Long Island, working under the guise of an Apple rep after flunking out of the Wharton School of Business. With such managerial prowess, it is no wonder Sharfstein has never set foot in the Congo and has no intention to.

Condon emails out another fast reply:

Dear Ms. Hainsey,

How do things find you in Libertyville? As a lifelong Bronx resident and erstwhile staffer at the Zoo, I've never been to Illinois, the birthplace of Lincoln. I hope you enjoyed your visit to New York. (Did you get to Arthur Avenue?) I want to express my deepest regret that your daughter was told what she was. No ten year-old should know that Connie Francis was raped at a Howard Johnson's. This is just not the kind of knowledge we at the Congo Forest wish to impart. Our docent will be dealt with forthrightly. Please let me offer you a free voucher should you wish to return . . .

There are many more emails to send. It will gobble up the brunt of his morning. He hates emailing fiercely, but it is a necessary trouble if Edith is to remain. These mornings have been his second lease, his third act, his last-inning grounder past the base. He still has to say it to believe it, a bubonic mantra: Sharfstein is my superior. Sharfstein is my boss. For months after his appointment Errol lumbered to work, blandly managed his docent roster, his very gibbons a reminder of being passed. Then one day Edith just turned up and asked to join the docent course. Within a week of passing, she came to him with revolutionizing notions the zoo might improve. He nodded, disconcerted; then, after her fourth unbidden tantrum when she told a woman she was Reubenesque "but not like the painting; like the sandwich," Errol began to warm to her barreling displays. He would never admonish her, never correct her; never interdict. He kind of even liked her.

Sometimes she has had "off-days," days where she sticks to her docent pages, saying nothing of controversy, and those days are very sad for Errol indeed.

Admittedly, he doesn't know much about Edith Frankel, only what the bolts of invective let go piecemeal, the grizzled torrents. He knows she had a husband named Norman who keeled over in Boca Raton while they were sitting by a pool reading their *Winds of War*. From what all Errol can gather, he was an undermining but faithful human being. She has a son named Martin who doesn't visit enough and has some landholding boondoggles drying in the sands of Arizona that have very nearly slammed him in the klink. She was bad at math and couldn't teach math so she became a social worker; that was ages back, pre-psychedelic U.S. She lives in a building near Mosholu that is now mostly Russians, of whom she has nothing very flattering to say. If her people had saints, she'd've put a shabbat candle under FDR's chair-bound portrait. She wears a mock monogram-Vuitton handbag she copped off a Fordham Road vendor. She wears cloche caps.

He types.

. . . *I must apologize mucho, Senorita Villalobos, that your visit was so malo, but my docent's cabesa don't work muy good. Milton Berle's pinga certainly has no business being hablad aqui.*

He hits Delete. He never learned Spanish, and knows he will have to auto translate this one.

Wonders of the modern world: auto translate. Megascreens. On the way in every day, he hauls ass past the 4-D Colossus, there menacing the Birds of Prey.

A purist, it is hard for Errol to stomach Sharfstein's proto-digital whistles and bells; his penchant for CGI inducements

17

when Man Small Beast Bigger as a wowing visual was there for the asking if you only got your ass on the Monorail. Sharfstein drips with new plans, though. Voucher offers, more touchscreens; considerable rollbacks in primates.

"Animals are a nuisance for a zoo," he said upon his appointment, Errol getting the full douche ramble in his office chair. "The risk quotient is brutal. Do you fight screens? Screens win. The kids could have a reanimated Pteranodon thumping around in the ape corral like one foot in front of them and move to find the beast on the fucking Kindle. 'Hey ma, Pteranodon!' The pixel ones do the genuine mud-flingers a ton better and you know it. Not like when you were a kid. Bogart sounded like some shortwave coming through an underwater fuzz box and was a monochromatic protagonist like they all were. You had to jack off your nut to a pursed lip kiss, am I right? That or a Botswanan tribeswoman's pendulous knockers bobbing over some rhino dung in a National Geographic your mom got so your brain would grow."

"I didn't watch Bogart growing up. I'm a little younger than that."

"A spring chicken you are not! Anyway, say sayonara to the quaint, Condon; pretty soon we'll all be shitcanned for a headset. We all know VR viewfinders are the coming wave. Kid'll strap on one and an ape will come barreling right up into his stunned grill. They'll have to defibrillate the little pissant from the coronary. Rack it, babe. My thoughts are so rad they deserve time stamps."

It is little consolation that Sharfstein is feared but not respected. He drives a Lamborghini Diablo replica. The one time he parked it on the street vandals broke in, ripped the seats out and turned them upside down, pinning a note to the dashboard that read, "Whatcha gonna do? Call the replica police on us?" He is ascendant, though. Growing, as colossal as the Le Pain Quotidien croissant that sits captivating buzzing horseflies on his work desk; for all its gadget gimmickry, modernity seems to be shot through with the animating principle of neglect.

Sharfstein will outlive Errol. He is young. Errol knows he should make way, clear out, pack south. Gregory Bullard from Marsupials owns a condo in the Yucatan that mostly survived the last named storm. But Errol has never had the wherewithal for that. He's always cursed darkness. It exacts less current from the grid.

A new email comes in, but it is not a complaint from a zoo-goer; it is Sharfstein.

The subject heading reads: "Heads up manana bubby tittie." Condon, sighing, clicks.

"So heads up manana as I said bubby tittie. Trackle and me are going to view the apes. Wants to see the docent. Stoop thinks your program rocks. Be there or be circle."

Errol quakes. Tomorrow; there will be little to no time to right the ship. He calls Edith, hoping to absent her, call in a humdrum ringer for the day, but she never answers her phone. He is never in any shape for Trackl but this is worse, *the* worst, a surefire axing. Trackl is a white-haired, rose-cheeked foundation donor whose dead wife is the posthumous christener of a good many namesake oncology wings, theater lobbies, zoo forests. He is a boorish man, but instrumental in repopulating the Congo's primate roster. No doubt he has come to look at what his funds have procured, to check in with Sharfstein, to smile unctuously as the latter eats his own tongue trying to express the worthy progress of the exhibit commensurate with the bounty he has got.

Errol tries Edith again. When the tempered birdsong of her non-answer beats into his phone eight times, the metronomic intervals of these rude rings spelling nothing less than the promise of certain death, he considers his position, his years caressing his tenure in this kingdom. Have the years been worth it? He has communed with the natural tucked away in a cement mausoleum that has claimed the headiest of his high school friends, streets that have devolved into chain outlets, crack dens, rubble. At least some friends got out, through a northbound blue bus to the penitentiaries, through dope, but what were Errol's options? A man schooled in the Passions, friend of Bronx boy iconoclasts who raided the aumbry at St. Clare's, he was told early by his mother Angie he was "wrong." Even though he never looked at women, was never caught concupiscent, even when Ed Solomon flashed that busty tomato nearly bursting out of her western house dress on the cover of *Hot Lead Trail*. It is just this kind of unjust circumscription from a mother that makes a grown man scramble for revenge; put an exclamation point on the hermitage of his life. Young Errol found his ecstasies in the cages, not the gospels. He grew full-hearted but single, a man habituated to unshared clutter. He has fostered and festered and fought. But an autopsy of Errol would show nothing but the accreted fats of his consolation meals, plaque from the marron glacés, no illicit substances, no marital heartache, just a curdling porridge of lukewarm payback. Just one old grousing yenta from Mosholu.

Maybe she's dead, he thinks; and that's why there's no

answer. No, she has never answered her phone. Who would call? Her son? He sounds like the last one who would. Edith, not surprisingly, has no cell phone. He'll intercept her, tell her of an asbestos problem; a Congolese microbe that piggybacked the transatlantic journey on an ape. Something will work. He will stay and fight. What would his papa, Daddy Tangiers, do? Fight? Flee? Probably neither. The man liked bebop jazz and Cuban cocktails, dancing the rhumba in white bucks. By 1959 he was a beatnik without a cafe, a reciter of Bill W. love psalms, jittering around street corners, waving over cars with the windows near-down, sealing friendships with a demonstrative palm clap that passed on his intimate secrets as the Ramblers blazed off screaming tracks to the Webster bypass, their drivers giddy with his bagged grams, then he was gone. Young Errol only knew his father ended his captivity on Earth by deteriorating of peritonitis in a Tangiers jail, chained to two men under the mud dome that passed for the hall of justice. When the State Department called a year later and said they had his body, he and his mother were unaware he had even been out of the States.

When they shipped his coffin back his mother had him cremated and threw the ashes down the ventilation shaft, where pigeons fled the upswell of his triturated marrow, the virile bullion that would expire with Errol's stunted drives.

Growing up across from the gate of the zoo, Errol could hear the lions in the morning, an urban reveille as routine as squab trills. He could hear those squabs too, confused, nativists inundated with strange Amazonian life; hotshots off cacophonous humidors like Madagascar, chiming from their palace The World of Birds. The pigeons would perch on the rooftops and wonder what these things were.

Errol knows he is a pigeon now, shrugging, grappling: Who are these new birds? What sad modern promotes the Eric Sharfsteins? Where does a man of his age go when the world is all 4-D, replicated Italian snazz-jobs, polymer headsets overloading your neuropathways faster than the coursing vein venom that attended his daddy's skin-pops; the world itself now a drug demanding full tolerance, a place so much bigger than it should be. Errol remembers his Edith:

Humans are the only animals to outlive their teeth.

She arrived early today. Errol intercepted her at the gate and told her asbestos was being cleared. She wasn't buying. He told her an ape was vomiting. She said, "What else is new?" Errol, after imploring her multiple times to leave, getting bullheaded stares and rancorous mutters for his efforts, finally tried the honest truth: Be nice, he told her. Stick to the script, the words on your docent pages. Pages, Edith, pages; no wandering off said script. She relented, unsure of what she had been doing wrong up till now, and took the packet. Errol spent the morning in the coffee room, drilling the words, testing the calcification of her memory, finding that, underneath the volatility, her mind was still robust.

Now she is standing by the triple-pane, a mandrill curled up in an unbothered slumber on the ape side of this fabricated colony. A trickle of morning guests has very quickly become a torrent. She is wearing a cathouse's panoply of rouge and seems chipper to be promenading among the guests. The gorillas knuckle to and fro in the fern grove, nose out the smallest alterations in their habitat, pawing spiky cones and straw gewgaws on the bunched grass. Edith gives Errol a thumbs up. He gives her one back. He sips his coffee like a football coach watching a blue-chip prospect running drills. The crowd lines up along the wall.

Sharfstein has come into the viewing area with R. Barry Trackl. Standing next to Trackl and clasping his chubby hand is a very tall drink of water, a vivid set of Cherokee angles for a face. In her lush Dior and white platforms, she makes her companion miniature.

Before Errol can say or do anything Edith steps forward, addressing the crowd that has formed.

"Ladies and gentlemen, now that you're here," she says, "do you want to hear about these apes?"

Some use their native language to indicate assent, others grunt, and the crowd steps closer to Edith.

In tones that are strangely halting, like a local linebacker doing a cable spot, Edith points and says, "That is an Eastern Mountain Gorilla. It hails from the volcanic mountain rangers of Central Africa, namely, and not coincidentally, given where your visit has taken you, the Democratic Republic of Congo." She flings her arm out animatronically at the Congo sign. "This gorilla is a descendant of the very first hominoid primates of the Oligocene Period. Its average weight is upwards of four hundred and thirty-some pounds. It is known to run up budding branches and forage grasslands for nutrients, hydrating carefully at the start of day. Hydration. That's water, people! And, our gorilla is diurnal. Which means it hunts and feeds during the day. A powerful animal, it uses signal displays to encourage its enemies to back off when encountering trouble in the vines. But, ladies and gentleman, do not let its posture fool you, it—is—no—slouch."

There are chuckles as perfunctory as the little scripted joke. Errol feels his heart steady now, the air fall under him like the cushion of bath beads. There are vague trepidations within those steady beats that keep Errol from believing what is in front of him: that this is really going off without a hitch.

He breathes in with Vinyasa-like ease.

Presently, Sharfstein motions for Errol to come over. Errol steps as though the floor panels will drop out from under him, but when he gets there Sharfstein is all smiles

"Errol, you remember R. Barry Trackl and his friend Oona Smalls."

"Yes. Right," says Errol, watching Edith buttonholing a Catalonian in the corner.

Trackl shakes Errol's hand, vicelike as one would expect.

"I was telling Barry about the docent program," says Sharfstein. "What a winner it is. *I told you, Errol!* I told you! Anyway Trackl here—"

"I'd like to meet your docent," says Trackl; his voice practiced in its obtuseness; the timeworn smokescreen of affect the rich have of always just being along for the ride. "I admire it when the community gets involved."

Errol nods, notes a rising column of pressed air bottlenecking at the base of his skull. He should have walked before Sharfstein, he knows. He should've cleared out years ago. He'd have gone to Tangiers with his father, joined up with the merchant marines. He'd have cooked up a record label, been a Phil Spector who didn't shoot. He'd have had Hollywood stunners with the gams of Daddy Longlegs in a stretch Continental spread across the fatty reaches of his abdomen.

The icebox of his coiled loins might well have thawed then. But, looking at the pathetic figure of Sharfstein with his showroom smile, the smug taper of his slim jeans over his cordovan Payless loafers, the shiny untucked button-down just barely kissing his waddly hips, that evil can be temporary, a snow job. He loves this place, its Benjamin Moore-scented office rooms, its landscape a dumping ground for history, and he is glad to have picked through the smoking ruins the curators have left him in the form of these erstwhile apes. He has ample faith it will keep him in its grip, that Edith is having one of her off days, that this last minute drilling of prefab shtick will provide him the cover he needs. Why just look at how she nailed that rap. The Catalonian woman she is talking to looks thoroughly edified, smiling not queasily, but with gratitude.

"Edith," yells Errol. He sighs and waves her over simultaneously. She comes shuffling across, happy to be wanted.

"Hello, people," she says. "Hello Mister Sharfstein!" She waves at him as though he were standing a mile away.

"Edith, this is R. Barry Trackl, one of our chief patrons," says Errol. "And this is Oona, his friend."

"Fiancée, actually," says Trackl. Oona lowers her face demurely.

"Whoa," says Sharfstein, reeling back and clapping his hands together and pounding his chest gorillalike. "Mazeltovs in the casa."

For a moment Condon feels relieved that Sharfstein might be the one who needs restraints. In these kinds of rickety exchanges there is often a designated idiot, and there is no rule that states it has to be the docent.

"Congratulations, Mr. Trackl; that's wonderful news," says Edith.

Edith's posture is reserved; she seems to have exerted command over the why-when-and-how of reality, the barest rudiments of equitable badinage as it plays. Yes, this is one of her off-days.

"You have a beautiful fiancée," she says, almost curtsying.

"Thank you," says Trackl. Oona, no doubt accustomed to such praise, fights a novel blush, receiving it from one so elderly.

"I'll bet I could cut glass with the shit-eating grin you must wake up with in the morning, looking over at *that*," says Edith.

"Ah," says Trackl, his smile still wake-riding the previous compliment, with only a few scant flutters at the sides.

"Well, Edith, we've got viewers," says Errol, taking her by the hand. "Very nice to see you all." Edith slaps his hand off.

"I'm talking," she says. "Don't you see I'm talking?"

Sharfstein flicks his eyes to the donor; a rosaceous man, it is difficult to know when he is blushing, but he appears to be bolding fast, unwilling to retreat from his admiration.

"You, uh, enjoy your work here at the zoo?" Trackl ventures.

"Oh yes. If I wasn't doing this I would be marooned, just out to lunch," says Edith. "I'm pretty much dead below the waist so I'm not going to be home getting my rocks off to some movie with Monty Clift in it. My bones are shit to the marrow and I can't afford Humira. I might as well become one of these poop-flingers with the sorry state of my hands being wrecked. People don't appreciate their basic blessings. This one standing here in the platform shoes, your betrothed, I'll bet you kiss the fucking toilet when she gets up. You *know* from blessings. You're so small they could bury you in your own ball sack, but here you've got this tree on your arm. No way this is your first rodeo with a wife."

"Edith, please," tries Errol.

"Mister Trackl's first wife passed away," says Sharfstein.

"Well I bet you're fuckin' glad about that!" says Edith, rapping a hand off Trackl's elbow and laughing. The man's flush is dramatic now, and Oona's readymade bonhomie has all but flown the coop. Trackl will be damned to cede his smile, but nods his head at a rate to suggest a new venue is dearly in the offing.

"You look Swedish," Edith says to Oona. "Are you Swedish?"

Oona simply shakes her head no.

"Why is it you Swedish women have some prominent teeth? Is it like something where you have to chew through the ice to get to the herring?"

"Is she always like this?" says Sharfstein to Errol, already helplessly miming "no."

"Oh I'm always very chummy with the apes," says Edith, reassuringly. "Mister Condon gives me good hours. He tells me I do wondrous. Every time I come in he might as well be handing me a flower bouquet. This place knocks me out; I want to come someday dressed like Jane from Tarzan, remember Maureen O'Sullivan, back with Weismuller and she wore that two piece? I'll have to rip off my corn pads but fuck it. I love the Congo. This is much better than the real Congo, with Belgian soldiers and AIDS. You know Reagan was a real asshole with that thing. He could've done something. AIDS took Gertrude

Sobel's nephew Leeman, who was very talented. He did a male-only fan-dancing number that Adele Blank found sick but I thought was very skillful. The music was unbearable, just clanging forks or some cockamamie xylophone contraption. But I adore our uncloseted humanity. We used to have a bonobo in, the ones that go gay when the mood hits. You know the redneck shitheels we get rolling in from south of the Dixon should get an eyeful of those fuckers going full-tilt, cornholing each other in this terrarium. Teach Ma and Pa Clampett a lesson. I have this idea, my little brainstorm, that all the bisexual gibbons get planted in a nice field and then, to the right of these red-asses, you Astroturf in another field that is a foundry with a work gang of big bald Polish morons breaking rocks, as naked as the *miserable day they were born!* Then you have this cuckoo clock like the one in Vienna and when that strikes the hour the Polish guys all drop their pickaxes and bang each other in the ass till their eyes go cross. It'll show the descent of Man. But I never liked Reagan, his acting. He was in a movie with a monkey. Until I was here I didn't know from animals. Bernice Krumholtz the knockaround did. She once brought home this baby duck. Thought it was darling, but what shit she had going on with it. Quack you into an unhearing person. And the fuckin' thing had to be in the bath all the time! It was a mess. But Errol is like a son. *He's a gift!* He always says 'you're doing great.' And backs me up if someone doesn't get my answers. And that's important. It's like what my father, who was a loser and should've gone into corrugated metal with his brother-in-law who became a mayor and a big time tomcat chasing after stage dancers in Piscataway, New Jersey — don't you know he died on a chorus girl from Dickie Waldmere's Footlight Ensemble while he was juking her caboose from behind and he slumped right on her and she thought he was taking a breather but he wasn't he was *dead* — used to say: You can catch more flies with honey. Errol catches those flies with me."

Edith, as though to indicate a full stop, smiles primly. Errol feels the room air congeal into a single blob of weighted molecules, the silence only pulling more atoms in.

"You wanna stay here for a minute?" says Sharfstein to Edith, finally.

Edith says. "Sure, Shitstain, I'll wait!"

"What?" says the latter.

"Ha! I know your name is Sharfstein but I like to call you Shitstain. You know," says Edith to Trackl, "Sharfstein here drives a Lamborghini that's about as real as your wife's tits."

Sharfstein leans over and is whispering in Trackl's ear but looking very squarely at Errol Condon. His eyes are very small and there is the shadow of a grin, the afterburn of a reckoning clear on his face: that of knowing the great squab of hope will die in roost before it even got the dry bread in its snapper. Errol looks at Sharfstein with a little smile and mimes a gun to his own head with his empty ring finger.

"Pow," he mouths.

Sharfstein nods, maybe even a little sadly.

Behind them, Edith has snuck away and is pressing her nose to the glass, meeting palms with a standing ape.

Errol bundles himself against November, but it is not so cold as that. He is going out to buy marron glacé off his remaining pension. He has few worries aside from time, which is more spacious now, a big skating rink for a man wearing flat-soled shoes. He can shuffle, though: no wife, no kids; some stories. He thinks of traveling, but there are no airports in the Bronx, and jetlag is alive in his body. After the episode they checked his computer and found the emails. He was cooked before but that tore it. When he heard Edith had been made a ward of the state and sent up to a remote Brooklyn hospital, bored and fading, by all rights, he felt a little sad, but she has walls, he imagines; tapioca by the wagonload, a rec room with a TV that affords her the catharsis of a haranguing court judge, any number of these robed strutters fairly studding the daytime lineup. She can watch an assortment of malfunctioning backwash try to finagle easy money from the world, the ripe red future of the hominid, production values, meth teeth, and a wallet that fattens with the February sweeps. It is better to shelter in place, away from the noble battle that will fail. He flips his collar up, fights the cool wind, and wonders if the apes know what is missing.

GLORIA (VIA)

"My features form with a change in the weather."
—Roland Orzabal

She caught your god in a river. She'd kick
the swirling thing and say *come
on, lobelia blue, stop leaning like
the hurricane never left your back.* And *you,*

the swirling thing would say, *come
closer: I am not yet drowned.* But
the hurricane never left. You're back and you
want some new myth, some new song called,

The Closer I Am. Not yet drowned, but
struggling against the current forcing you to
want some new myth, some new. A song called
out to you from an old radio and crackled

struggling against the current, forcing you to
try to remember the words, the wanting to get
out. To you, from an old radio, crackled
the voice that washed you new in the eye of it.

DINOSAURS AMONG US

after an exhibit at the American Museum of Natural History

Mounted on an exhibition wall I see
a vestigial bone or rather, a card of bones,

translucent wishbones of 13 kinds of birds
circling that of *Tyrannosaurus rex*, the progenitor,

like the immaculate surround of saplings
born of the central sarsaparilla tree.

The furcula. It holds a sacred place
in wakeful childhood, granting the well-behaved

the permission she was forever prone to seek;
and even then, the wish was purely binary:

big half, small half, yes/no, fervent hope
fulfilled or dashed. One found it best to make

desultory wishes one didn't care about.
And looming in the center of that life

the overpowering overhang of grownups,
listing all the powers I'd never have

until maturity, or decades enough that I might
pretend to that exalted pinnacle.

How did I get here? That dino bone feels like me,
bogged and leaden, surpassed by twittering birds.

ODE TO A TRAFFIC LIGHT

My tricolored beauty, it's you
I rely on in the lax mornings

in my lukewarm murmurings
of indecision. Precisely as
a metronome, you adjudicate
the crossroads
where yes meets no,
where stay meets go
and now meets soon.

Your citrine caution compels me
to carve out a moment,
weigh my wanderlust
against the probity of pondering.

While waiting for
your emerald prompt,
I regard your steady ruby eye
and ask myself whether it's right,
at least here,
to angle for advantage.

Do I dare turn right on red?

My lifesaver,
I love when you choose
for me. It's tantamount
to caring.

STRIKE CITY

Here she existed last week until she vanished in her dress, dragged from a weedy edge of the parking lot behind the bank after her shift. No, not married. No, no kids. No cash on her person, cell phone dead, a petal-pink 9mm in her purse. See, there she is on the news, the CCTV footage, fingers gripping the driver's-side door before a man strikes her head and roughs her away. See her keys fall, a chunk of light like you rubbed your eye, and that's it: no suspects, no leads, summer coming anyway, and this rotten place reeking of blossoms that smell like sex, disgusting or fragrant depending on which way you turn your head.

Here in Strike City she smiles like she's alive on highway billboards and I can't escape her, not at the bar where I work, not at home where my inherited parrot apologizes in Spanish, not in the sideways downpour that soaks my dress, wrecks me up. Rain is the reason I duck into the art museum, its doors tomb-heavy and the marble floors singing like the moments before a funeral. These days I wait for someone to hand me a candle. For the vigil to begin.

And it's just a moment later when it happens, the next violent thing in under a week: the sound is a rip, and after the rip there's silence, and I'm not even a little dry yet and nobody breathes. I think *dress* when I hear it, picture a man tearing a woman's skirt up her thigh. But it's actually a painting. Not clothing, but canvas. Yes, someone has sliced a huge square of simple pink and red, and now a knife lies on the ground and my umbrella drips on the floor and the white marble statue in front of me is a woman with her eyes closed and a hand to her ear likes she's listening. Well, I could tell her some things.

Because then the actual surprise comes, even though it shouldn't be one: the creep in all-black pushes me, his hairy hand shoving my chest before he runs out into the storm. My brain doesn't have time to register his face, to make sense as I nearly slip, to make my mouth push words out.

But because I'm soaked to my skin and this place felt sacred a moment ago and I have nothing to do on this day off besides clean out my deceased mother's apartment or feed her parrot or clean the parrot's ridiculous heart-shaped cage, and because I'm sick of the many things men in this world get away with, I run after him. Outside it's sun-raining, sheets coming down without clouds and the heat mucking up dead cicadas, the stink and steam rising around me as I pant. I run hard, and believe me when I tell you I get so close I touch his back. I like to believe he had gooseflesh on his neck. *I'm so close* is what I think the moment before my foot twists and he slips away over the wet hill.

The Bar is the bar where I work, though I don't drink these days, not at all, because I like to keep my wits, like to stay laced-up and ready to leave if I need to, ready to drive, because the world is no place to be without a plan, a brain, a car. At the start of my shift, it's just me and the Budweiser girl from St. Patrick's Day, a life-sized cardboard cutout with her belly bared, perfect innie, and a shamrock painted on her face. I would say we have an understanding, though she never says a thing, not even about the fact that this place used to be a funeral parlor and that the owner Mick who lives upstairs once saw his dad laid out on what's now the bar. "Right here," he'll say and he'll slap his hands on the wood and show you where.

No one to serve yet, nothing to polish or mop because these are the slow, clean evenings of summer when the nearby campus is empty and when the regulars trickle in later, everyone moving at half-speed through bugs and blossoms and heat, so I turn the television on and, between game shows, I find the local news, which one might expect to feel less dire than the national news, but here we are: picketers pushing back, green-winged cicada plague, painting vandalized at the museum, woman still missing. No bank account activity, no cell phone pings, no leads.

I want to call a friend or my brother or my mother – the latter being an impulse that will never leave me – but this secret I hold inside might sour the precise moment I share it with another. So let me say it to you, at least: I don't know how I know this, but I know that the man who kidnapped the woman at the bank is the man from the museum. I've never had a psychic sense, could never predict a thing, but at home, this thought has me twisting in my sheets. I can't sleep for the tingle in my fingers, the fight-or-flight chemicals flooding me.

"Lo siento, lo siento," the parrot says in the dark without a trace of pity. "Time to leave," he says. And he may be right about me being done with Strike City. But first I have to find this guy who's alive outside, allowed to be in the world where cicadas multiply themselves, their husks flooding gutters and their buzzing making it hard for any of us to think.

"Look like someone will miss you," my mother used to say about how not to get kidnapped. Her generation of women has advice for mine—on how to dress or drink or carry our keys—but when I return to the museum the next afternoon, I actually do what she said: I look like a woman who's coming or going, like a woman you're waiting for, and I wear it well, I think, this look of purpose. As I walk through the corridor, I think I should pretend it's my lunch break. My mother used to drive home on her own lunch breaks to water overgrown geraniums along the backside of her apartment building. The flowers weren't even hers. Then she'd go inside and feed the parrot pieces of mango and let him out of his cage, that bird a silly impulse-purchase because she thought she'd live a long time, or maybe because she knew she wouldn't.

The space where the man sliced the work of art is blank. I sit on a bench facing the white wall where the pink and red canvas hung. I've learned all about the missing woman's life on the internet, found her Facebook profile, her New Year's Eve smile with the champagne flute in her raised hand. I even know the street she lived on from the TV news feeds' broadcasts from her neighborhood. And it's not just me, because the town can't stop about her, either: people pin pink ribbons to lapels, lamp-posts, trees, all of it a signal that she's real, still existing. I have few beliefs, but I believe that the man will come back here to the museum and I will be ready to catch his throat this time, to scratch his hairy hand as I take him down.

The wall blurs and fuzzes, looks less white the longer I stare, and I see some faint scratches in the coat of wall paint, and where is he hiding her? This place is empty except for the security guard whose heels click-click as she rounds this mausoleum. She and I are surrounded by the dead in the form of glossy oil crucifixion scenes and the Egyptian sarcophagus and the silk and watercolor and clay and string: natural materials decaying before my eyes as I sit and wait. I'm outnumbered by ghosts.

Which is why I startle when the guard leans down behind me and asks "What are you doing?" She whispers it in my ear, and the closeness of her mouth sends prickles down my back and all I can say in a barely-there voice is, "I like this piece." I point to the painting next to the blank spot, a still life of wilted peonies and bees in a heavy gold frame. Meanwhile, my heart does double-time, the same feeling I get when a cop gives me a ticket.

But she sees through me, and it's clear that she's watched me long enough to know why my gaze was fixed on a blank wall. "It was expensive," she bends to tell me, breathing on my neck. "A rare one," she whispers and shakes her head like it's a shame, even though she's kind of smiling. She and I are the same age and I don't know why, but I always look at ring fingers and hers is empty. Her skin is pale, probably from being indoors in this very still, quiet place all day long and let me tell you: I'm not used to being confided in outside the four walls of the bar and I take it as my sign to leave.

I guess what makes me drive there is the same fascination I have with roadside crosses dotting highways and their silk flowers growing shabby in the sun. Why I scan obituaries over coffee if I'm up early. Why I slipped away and walked two miles to the bridge after my neighbor leapt to her death in the frozen river. My mother used to warn me not to go so dark, but my hands steer the car toward the parking lot of the bank, which isn't far at all, barely a detour, and anyway: no one would know if it weren't for my telling you. I just want to understand what can't be understood so at least I can say that I tried.

People walk into the bank and people exit the bank, though I can't say anyone rushes or hurries. There's no urgency to the day for the gray man in the gray suit or the mother lifting her baby from a sedan's backseat. I park and walk along the concrete sidewalk to the back of the bank, the bigger lot where employees park. Asphalt crumbles and parking lines fade and, behind the blacktop, a row of old brick homes are being divvied into apartments by gentrifying landlords. I look around the parking lot hoping to find a hair pin, a penny, a message, but there's nothing and the fact of it comes as a surprise.

As I walk the length of the lot looking for what doesn't exist, I see a thin woman writhing in a second-story apartment window, no shirt on, her hands pressed against the glass, her lips parted, eyes closed. And I don't want to watch, don't mean to for so long, but it takes more than a moment to understand what's happening — this pale, naked figure moaning in the window — and then it takes a moment longer to parse the silhouette of a shirtless man moving behind her, and then another moment after that to feel shame for looking at what they wanted me to see, were hoping I'd see. *Lo siento* I think and there's the electricity in my belly again. The truth, I promise, is that it surges even before she opens her eyes, notices me standing below, and closes her lips into a smile.

I like Strike City less and less as each day passes without the dead coming back, but what really does it is the Budweiser girl. Because as I flick on the lights at the start of my shift that night, I see that someone has taken a black sharpie to her and scrawled devil horns on her head and pubic hair across her cheerleader skirt and scratched over the shamrock and onto her mouth the words "Nick's Bitch." I don't know Nick, and I don't know who did this, but under the amber glow of the lights I carry her to the back of the bar. It's not that I ever really liked her and, anyways, March is long-gone, but I feel a little ill throwing her in the dumpster as evening eases itself into this shitty town.

There are woods and there are seas. Besides the parrot: nothing I'd need to take with me. "You can catch a fish," my mother would say and shrug like, what more do you need? I can sleep to new night sounds besides buzzing. The pink ribbons will be bleached and frayed by September and who needs to be there to see it? Not me. There will be no homecoming. *Time to leave.*

The bar smells like lemons because Mick must've been polishing the wood. The jukebox is clean, too—no fingerprints—and the pool tables are ready for the regulars to talk shit across them. If you didn't know better, you might think this place is a church just before the doors open. Green and glass and brass and perfectly still. So, I suppose I will miss it or maybe just the certainty of what's inside The Bar: a bar, which somehow makes more order in the world, not less of it, the way people might think.

By nine-thirty the sun has settled behind some mountain range no one knows the name of and a college guy plays the same band on repeat and small clusters of people off work late or people with no work at all talk loudly over the speakers and one another. And it's the noise I'm thinking of when I spot her leaned over a two-top and staring at me, right at me, almost through me, really, with a sharp, dark glance and her mouth to a beer glass. When she sees me notice her, her eyes narrow with a little laugh in them. The security guard is here and she has found me.

There are two kinds of people, my mother would say, and I don't even remember how she'd finish that, but I realize it might be true: there are people who do and people who watch, the inside people and those on the edge of the circle. And who's to say which is luckier, really? Because you can be on the camera or watching the camera footage on the news. You can be naked in the window or looking up at the window from the street. I know where I am in all of this which is where the security guard is, too, even though she's not wearing a uniform and is just a regular woman now, a woman who followed me here maybe, a woman in a black dress with a purse over her shoulder.

Goodbye, Budweiser girl, and so long to my mom's dead geraniums and thank you, maybe, to the parrot who'll likely live longer than all of us. The security guard will stay at the bar for two hours, never walking over to order from me but sending a man instead to get beers two at a time, and who knows if he's her boyfriend or a stranger but his hands are rough as he presses bills into my own more than once. A week from now, they'll find the missing woman's cell phone and pink gun with its paint chipped, both artifacts pressed in mud near the river, all of it the signs we've been waiting for, though the wrong ones. The next day, her family will weep at a press conference and the red and pink painting will stay stored for years until the museum finds a patron with money enough to fix it.

But before all that, there's tonight, and tonight on this walk home from the bar for the final time, the cicadas fly in their reckless, knee-high circles, spinning themselves dizzy before crashing into the ground. They were never meant to live long—a single summer at most—and they can't defend themselves against predators. Their survival is sheer numbers: they may be fragile but the world can't kill them all.

NATURAL SELECTION

Wisdom teaches that birds in the house mean death.
If you leave the flue open, they'll flutter down
the chimney. Sometimes you can smoke them out
while other times you cannot. Termites are obvious.
The elephant in the living room is less so.
Although we rarely discuss it, there is a sense
that domestication is the fourth miracle we seek
in an order that goes: water, fire, food, shelter.
For cats and dogs it must be strange to imagine things.
Larger versions of themselves would eat the humans
who scoop dry chow into their bowls. They must,
from time to time, sit in the window after tonguing
themselves clean and see the neighborhood strays
wandering the night blackened street. They must have
etiquette.   They must have superstitions
so painfully consistent the only word for it is religion.

CANON

1

Were I to start   for example
a well-intentioned list of objects
pertaining to injustice

*green card   Trinidad   suitcase
notebook*   it would remain
to point out the only

way I have of understanding
is to say *ships* gathering
momentarily in the crook

of a bay   (or maybe
some might call them
vessels)   very far away

2

I'd hoped as we aged
some sensitivity would emerge
but things got worse   I remember
how surprised I was Dostoevsky
devoted most of his journals
to ways to improve Russia
rather than his own problems
My poetry acquaintances
are so competitive   We don't
appreciate the meaning of great art
only the air-conditioned
hallways leading us handsomely
onto the frames   My poetry
I admit   is pretty institutional
aiming for the cushy
anthologies on which I was raised
School had duck ponds and white
stucco outside the classrooms
where   over the summer
the journalism teacher hosted
a *Brothers Karamazov* reading group
for interested students of which
there were many   The more
I try to be aware   the more
I care about prizes and awards
no matter how elitist
their history   I like the idea
of people reading my poems

and that I will one day be able
to perform that little dismissive
hand gesture at the mention
of everything I've won   I don't know
which I'd choose if I had to

3

Poetry gets ugly
when discussed with the wrong
people   No *you've* got the sunset
stuck in your eye
Pluck it out then talk to me
about how best
to christen literature
Tough to accept my most
weighty contribution
is to sit and listen
The earth has tilted :
every story I thought I'd tell
lost like a disc in the ocean
The argument   for example
that I did nothing personally
but purchase a field
with the clearest vista
the most utilitarian hay
There's what I represent
and then the way I've lived
both in a bottle of oil
in dark multiple
cabinets at once
Why shouldn't I love
Oedipus at Colonus
or the island where it's set?
Why shouldn't I tour its beaches
for their beauty alone?

G.J. Sanford

HOW TO LOSE CUSTODY

I've never felt
sand like this:
so sweetly heavy,

pushing back in a light spring
against my child's feet,
the bounce of flesh

of hands wide as villages
holding precious lakewater
in their soft desolate bowl

around which we make a circuit;
my son's hand in mine.
He is a brief infant

of light, marveling at the sudden shadow
of clay crawling between toes,
appalled and delighted

by the call of the dark
water lapping deceptive
at our ankles.

In my off hand bleeds
a half bottle of beer and he knows
but lets it pass —

the blind faith all children
profit and suffer from.
I know his eyes could

read me something monstrous
if they wanted to, but when I chainsmoke
on the way to the grocery store

he lifts his nose to the blue conversation
that billows around us and just
turns his head to the window

to contemplate the swirling kaleidoscope
of lawns as we pass. He allows me a freedom
I've never had, a lack of judgement

not usually afforded to people like me. So today
we chose the lake instead of summer camp,
to fling shit in the face

of whoever knows best. We *are* the shit-
flingers, the fatherless, and I wish
I could run naked down the shoreline

as if I were complete and alone, but the booze sneaks up
as usual, and I worry that if I leave him now
he will never think to wonder why.

YOUR LIFE IN AIRPLANE RIDES

1974

Your first flight is on Pan Am. You are four years old, en route to Caracas, Venezuela. You wear your best clothes, because everyone dresses up to fly, and it is exciting and glamorous. Your father has been transferred to Venezuela to help design large hydroelectric projects. Your parents had to go to the public library to look up Venezuela in an atlas after they had already agreed to go. The stewardess hands you an airplane wing pin that you stick yourself with, drawing a drop of blood.

1976

You are on a very, very long trip to Taipei, Taiwan, to meet your grandparents for the first time at age six. You sit with your family in a five-seat middle row, next to a nice man. Your mom, dad, and sister have fallen asleep and your neighbor offers you salty baked watermelon seeds. You take them even though you've been warned not to accept gifts from strangers. It will be the first, but not the last, time you disregard your parents' advice about strange men.

LATE 1970s

A few years later, you and your sister discover a delightful game with airplane meals. You mix the powdered cream with water and throw in salt, pepper, and gravy from your egg dish. You smear the concoction on a bun and dare each other to eat it. You begin a tradition that you will enjoy for many years to come but your kids will never experience in this age of meal-less domestic flights.

1986

You are sixteen, flying to Amsterdam on a class trip to the Model United Nations with seventeen of your closest friends, rivals, classmates, secret crushes, and two chaperones. It is KLM in the mid-80s, so they serve Heineken to high school students and flying is a cocktail party in the air—passengers stand around the aisles smoking, drinking, and chatting. Your group plays drinking games with the stewardesses. Your chaperones sit as far as they can from your group, sipping their wine and chatting.

On the second leg of the class trip, you travel to the Soviet Union at the height of the Cold War. You experience the terror of flying Aeroflot, on what seems a World War II relic. The seat backs flop completely forward. The flotation vests are canvas army-issued contraptions with light bulbs screwed to the shoulders. The wind whistles through the door. When you land in Moscow, you wither a bit under the dead-eye stare of a Soviet military officer scrutinizing your face and passport photo. You vow not to fly Aeroflot again if you can help it.

1987

Your family visits a colleague's farm in the interior of Venezuela. You survey his holdings in a private plane that just fits your family and your host. He shows you how he owns all the land that you can see from the air, horizon to horizon. You visit with the ranch hands. They explain how they have great lives, working with the animals and the land in return for free housing and job security from the *patrón*.

One week later, your host is hijacked on the same plane, forced to fly to Colombia to be ransomed by his family. Your host manages to escape the kidnappers: as they cross a river by horseback, he stabs the horse during the crossing to create a ruckus, allowing him to flee through the jungle and back across the border. You wonder whether you could have done the same thing if the plane had been hijacked one week earlier with your family on it. You decide you are not made of that kind of mettle.

1987 – 1991

During college, you fly back and forth between school and Caracas to visit your family on breaks. Because you are young and not jaded and because personal devices do not exist yet, you have conversations with your seatmates. Some of the people you meet include:

A rough and tough woman who is an office manager coming back from a visit with her fiancé, a sports photographer in New Jersey. She drinks throughout the trip, swears, hates vegetables, and doesn't eat the lasagna. At the end of the flight, the little kid in front of you turns to look at you and says to his mommy, "I think that lady likes me." When the kid and his mother are barely out of earshot, your companion declares loudly, "I hate kids."

An educator coming from a conference. She is a kindly woman eager to give life advice to a college student. She enjoys her drink. The two of you talk about the declining state of American education. She decries the growing gap between the wealthy and the poor.

On the way back from Caracas, a funny, friendly Venezuelan lawyer. You and she giggle the whole trip because she just has that kind of laugh. You talk about the differences between Venezuelan and American law. She's been on a five-day spending spree where she shopped from 10 a.m. to 10 p.m., went back to the hotel, stayed up watching TV, slept, rinsed and repeated. She has bought a microwave oven, several copies of computer software, and items that add up to way more than the allowable $1,000, so she spends a significant portion of the trip going through her receipts and her customs declaration, all the while giggling with you. Sadly, you know this would never happen now, as there is nothing to buy in the falling-apart-country-that-is-Venezuela, where visitors are the ones bringing in things like toilet paper and antibiotics.

1991 – 1997

Not for the first time, you look out the window and think about boundaries. Flying on the thin edge of land and sky, you find yourself in the In Between. In between the start and the finish, the origin and the destination, in the limbo of your journey.

In these six years after college, you cross back and forth over the continent as you study and live in Massachusetts, Hawaii, California, and Washington, D.C. Your job titles are law student, summer clerk, law clerk, and trial attorney. Your life titles are daughter, sister, best friend, girlfriend, fiancé, and wife. You fall in love with island living and the West Coast, but you return to plant roots in the East. You live the upwardly mobile American dream of professional responsibility, but you secretly wish to paint, draw, and write. Each time you study the changing landscape below, you reflect on borders, time, space, and memories past and ones yet to be.

1993

When you land at night into Maiquetía International Airport, the twinkling lights dotting the mountainside separating the coast from the capital beckon like stars in a mysterious universe.

You fly into Venezuela with your boyfriend from law school so he can meet your parents. You land in the day and see your home with new eyes. The mountainside of starlight is revealed to be covered by *ranchitos*, ramshackle tin-roof and brick hovels. The shacks are ubiquitous, packed all along the mountainsides of Caracas. Housing the poor — the majority of the city — the shacks cling to the mountains, occasionally washed down with the torrential tropical rains. They pose a stark contrast to the skyscrapers, high rises, tony homes, and golf courses in the city's valley — the Caracas you knew growing up. You remember how you tried not to dwell on the daily contradictions between the mountainsides and the valley.

Flying back to the States after a successful visit (marred only by a bout of intestinal distress when your boyfriend forgot his strict precautions and brushed his teeth with tap water), you do not realize that you will never see your home in person again. Your next aerial view of Caracas will be virtual when you find your apartment building on Google Earth, and more recently, when you see photos of protests and smoke bombs on your friends' social media feeds.

1997

It's your honeymoon, and the guide at your lodge informs you that you can't leave Zambia as scheduled because an attempted coup has shut down the airport. The next day, you decline the receptionist's request to carry a mysterious package out of the country. You and your spouse bounce along a road to the airport and are handed over to strangers to hop on the back of a pickup truck at a dusty and deserted intersection. You spend hours at the airport battling crowds and waiting in lines to finagle a seat out of the country.

Finally, you follow a man who takes you to an airplane the size of a large SUV, the last flight out of the country that day. You are the only passengers. The plane consists of the pilot seat and three seats. The pilot twists backwards and looks over his shoulder to back up onto the runway, as if backing out of his driveway. He asks your spouse to hold the door slightly ajar to keep you cool and yank it close only as you start down the runway. The pilot explains you must land in Zimbabwe by sundown because they have no landing lights. You pass the flight in partial whiteout conditions and find a magazine in the seat pocket in front of you entitled, "Flight Training." You land in Zimbabwe ten minutes after sunset, with just enough natural light to land.

SEPTEMBER 11, 2001

You are not flying this day, but your experience flying will always be divided between Before and After. Before, when you could walk up to a gate to greet a friend or your husband.

Before, when romantic comedies could rely on a dramatic airport reunion scene unencumbered by airport security. After, when you must prostrate yourself to the gods of TSA, with offerings in the form of three-ounce toiletries in plastic baggies, belts, laptops, and shoes.

On this day, the fulcrum between the Before and After, you are at a meeting a block from the White House when the first planes hit the World Trade Center. You manage to reach your husband, who is on a business trip in Manhattan, to find out he is safe.

When the plane hits the Pentagon, you realize you must leave the area around the White House. Six months pregnant, you walk ten blocks to your office, in a scene you never could have imagined: smoke billows from the Pentagon to the South; cars jam the streets; and people walk and stare in horror and fright. This is the only time you are ever actually scared that something might hurtle down upon you from the sky.

You wonder what kind of world your unborn child will meet. You feel a real sense of despair that things will never be the same again.

2001 – 2005

Your first flight with a baby at the end of 2001 is surprisingly easy, because your one-month old only sleeps and eats and has pipsqueak cries.

When your daughter is two years old, you give her a cashew from the airline snack pack. She immediately cries, her lips balloon, and she throws up over the man next to you. You learn two things: (1) she is extremely allergic to nuts (which sets you on a trajectory of doctors, Epi-Pens, a visit to the ER, and other stressful parenting moments), and (2) an extremely effective way to get an empty seat next to you and a toddler.

When your family adds another child, you are now an expert at traveling with a full complement of gear: car seat, stroller, diaper bag, books, toys, Ziploc bags, hand wipes, and many extra changes of clothing, for both you and your children. Tablets and smart phones have not been invented, so you do not have the benefit of built-in babysitters as you exhaust yourself wrangling a baby and toddler. You vow never to roll your eyes at traveling families and their young children again.

Present Day, 2017

You board a plane and greet the attendants. You find a spot for your roller bag, usually many rows from your seat, while taking care not to bump passengers with your over-full shoulder bag. From long habit, you count the number of rows to the nearest exit. You ignore the safety talk, even though you know that you shouldn't.

You are on your way to visit your in laws, or your parents, or a family vacation. The cabin is quiet, lights are dimmed, and passengers' faces are lit by phones and tablets, ear buds snaking from their ears. Each person is lost in their own world of Netflix, solitaire, a game, a sitcom, a thriller, or a book. You do not notice how anodyne, antiseptic, and antisocial traveling by plane has become, because you are busy reading on your phone.

You don't remember the last time you looked out the window of a plane at the land you are leaving, crossing, or coming to.

FLYING IN

First there's an ocean, a big left turn,
then mountains, desert, brown-blue haze,
a rift valley, oil wells, crop circles,
rivers with fingers, with feathers,
with nerve ends stroking hills, clouds,
walls of humidity, and then you, on the ground,
touchable, strokable, your professorial khakis,
red silk underneath, your layers of motivation
that protect you from desire, overcome
like distance in this age of easy travel,
I've come on real wings to take you home.

MUSING ON ARITH LOST TO TIME

Grandaddy's mother birthed 12 children
by 12 discrete men. I asked what she did
for work, and my big brother of a different father
laughed at my insinuation
that sex could be her job.
As if being a whore is a joke, a lark,
as if she, a ground-dwelling songbird
with her streaky brown plumage,
didn't shift her bones to shape the world
12 times. It was America after all.
It was 1930 to 1953. It was Beaufort,
South Carolina, and a woman
is her own business. What's so funny?
How many times did she make the shape of the sky
with her legs, the oblong sphere of the earth
with her belly? How many times was she an ossuary?
Arith with her crooked feet
maybe could only deliver her song
in flight, crest pressed forward by her back's arc,
belly swollen from fucking in that good
sweet way women do when they want to
feel goose-skinned, full, slick.
Arith. Everybody called her Mother.

EPITHALAMIUM

for Heather and Matt

The summer shower pauses and the sun comes out; it really does.
Cash sings of fever and the couple interlock their arms,

lift their beers to their lips. On the table, the ubiquitous cow skull,
its mouth spouting marigolds. We ten between summer showers,

laughing next to the pies, the blackberry torts. A wish:

nights of lucidity. Mornings in which you turn
and find him there, seeing you. A wish:

Can't we ask for anything? Good health. In lieu, celebrate
    your wedding
day, the sun and rain of it, the skull and flower. And kiss

with your eyes open, then closed. For safe travel back home,
my friend. Heather, canning rhubarb for the long winter

into spring. Matt, trapped in front of the bathroom mirror,
faucet running, hands covered in soap at his side.

Go home happy to sleep and wake to warmth
and morning breath. Now, Matt a little less himself.

His mother undressing him, guiding him to the shower.
Which parts belong to his wife? Bluebirds carry a white sheet, a

gurney's tinkling song. Matt's too long stare. Cow skull, its mouth
spouting marigolds. At the backyard wedding, the hydrangea

all grown back since the fire, the bride in blue and cowboy boots.
Celebrate the moment of unflinching honesty. A sincere,

everyday love there in the backyard. Everybody with
a chair and a story.

MS. TINA, THE FRANKFURTER LADY

A buck ten. She pushes her cart
up the stairs to her apartment.
Aluminum drawers jangle as she humps,
shoulder pressed to stairwell
wall, palm pressed to the cart's undercarriage.
She pushes it like a stalled car. Her
knees gain water as her hip gains
purchase. Next week she'll find
a garage. Tonight the cart
will wait against the rail dividing
the kitchenette from the dining table.
Tina, in her new post
"dismissed-with-cause" career
will sleep on the couch.
Her daughter has taken the bed.
And in the morning, begging help
from no one, she will set up shop.
She will back down the stairs.
Four floors. Calf then calf, toe then toe,
thump-clanking step by step
toward the street door and push her buns
and hot water tray up Rockaway
to the Brookdale Hospital doors.
She'll post her permit, *vendor*

number 33871, SIMPSON, E.
and ready her mustards with gloveless,
wrinkling hands in the rising sauerkraut steam.
She'll wait for the waiting room dwellers,
the nurses, the EMTs, the doctors,
the interns, the infirm to swarm the cart.

VERBS

Two miles into my walk
the word *be* appears on my tongue,
a short verb that seeds dream,
that creation, in its unundersatndable
domain, seems to know well,
to be, not to be and to be again,
the somethingness of existence.
Crow in sumac watches with keen eyes.
Oak leaf on the grass with sharp
points says pin oak, its name—
how the world worded itself
into existence is human, is bird,
is tree—each with its own sense
of being. Fungus and mold
make a home for oak roots,
say thank you for sugar in return.
And I, in my own impatience,
let pass what is life in each moment.
I'll try to make this a *Be* walk
until my mind flashes back
to England, Vermont, Idaho,
Virginia, or even a small mountain
creek named Laurel that flows
into the North River in Tennessee,

once a native trout stream until
road construction opened
a bauxite deposit that killed it;
what we remember once was.
I notice the orange-spotted
head of a tortoise beneath
yellow coreopsis —
both flowers of sorts —
the morning itself
a blossom. Be and
Was and Will Be.

ST. SIMONS MORNING I

Gandolf beards of Spanish moss
drape live oaks that shade village streets.

I steer my bike in zags to avoid hitting
swifts and lined skinks hunting the walk

for insects. Late June humidity molds
the skin, darkens my shirt with wet—

neck, back, armpits—Atlantic breeze
blocked until I turn on Ocean Blvd.

Palmetto scrubs grow in patches. All
this life formed long before humans

shaped earth's future toward disaster.
I let this thought rise and disappear

like rainbow bubbles children blow
in the park as the sound of waves

rushes the shore, wind flapping wings
of grackles and gulls dancing salty air.

Ancient Jains said *the way to liberation*
and bliss is to live a life of harmlessness.

Perhaps, in the beginning, first humans
learned the words *to be*, the future humans,

to breathe.

THE LIFE AND TIMES OF DEMI GEIST, AS TOLD BY HER DAUGHTER

My mother's grandfather could hold his breath for twenty hours. She told me once that he arrived on a great ship that sailed from England because he had been pressed into service. Salt from the sea spray stiffened his lungs like starch. Each day, he twirled his whiskers and watched the flotsam swirl around schools of shrimp. He kept his fingers nimble by weaving together frayed ends of rope. He swept the deck until his shoulders were knotted and he forgot what softness was like. One day he pushed his broom off the side and tumbled after it. He expected "Man Overboard" to be sounded, but nothing came. He expected to feel his tongue grow thick as he struggled for air, but kept swimming. Eventually, he turned into a little wrinkled thing suspended in the middle of sea. He held fast to the anchor and studied the ship's barnacle-encrusted bottom until the chain began to move. He considered letting it pull him up but he released it in time for the ship's current to carry him to a nearby bayou.

~

My mother once had tea with the nutria. When the backyard fig tree was heavy with fruit, she put on her gloves and carried her bucket to the place where the branches met the ground.

She plucked delicate orbs and put them in egg crates so they wouldn't bruise. A small animal beckoned among the roots. It could have been a snake but my mother was unafraid. Since the earth was nice and pliable, the nutria invited my mother to visit. She crawled underground (taking care to remember the figs) and found a cozy sitting room with a latticed ceiling. The nutria gave her dandelion tea in an acorn and asked her many refined questions on art and politics. My mother thought the nutria's voice was velvety and beautiful, unlike her father's salty tongue. She considered staying with the nutria, but remembered how her grandfather had turned down the monocle-wearing shrimp that invited him to live underwater, and she knew she belonged above ground. When they finished their tea, my mother complemented her host on its fashionable coat, and now the nutria lets my mother borrow it whenever she goes to the Orleans Parish Fur Festival.

~

My mother is heir to a whiskey fortune. She keeps a bottle of Cuttysark for special occasions. You'd never know she was wealthy because she likes to shop for brass candlesticks at Goodwill because they remind her of home. She tells me we can paint them with chalk gathered from the English sea. She shows me pictures of Dover and their whiteness startles me. The painted candlesticks look white but are blue in certain light. I ask her if it bothers her that the colors change, but she tells me that they help her remember the way home after she leaves. To me the flames look like gathering plankton on a moonlit night. Whenever she feels homesick, she calls her friends with a whiskey in hand and tells them how to fight evil. I imagine her at home, standing on a chair to reach the whiskey bottle on top of the fridge and licking the salty water from her lips when she's done.

~

My mother's parents once faced down a hurricane. They sat on their front porch eating red beans and rice until the tide came in. Once a car came by and offered to take them away. They answered no, and said "God will provide." The nutria stopped on its way out of town and offered to make amends. They declined politely but offered to share their meal. They picked at the last sausage casings as the hurricane's eye hovered closely. They stared it down until the hurricane turned green, then red with embarrassment and introduced itself. Since they were out of shrimp, they asked Audrey to stay for the pecan pie they had made for dessert. We can't visit their house anymore because it is mostly underwater. Sometimes the tide leaves long enough for us to see them sitting in their rocking chairs, their legs stretched out like a cat on the deck of a ship.

~

My mother likes: sorghum, figs, magnolia, green tomatoes, red pepper, garlic, boudain, nutria, *Leptoglossus gonagra*, candlesticks, shrimp, whiskey, seaweed.

My mother hates: cats, hurricanes, Pomme Wonderful, the dark.

~

My mother visits me twice a year on the solstice because she says it is the most hospitable time for ocean-dwellers. She travels by road, although she prefers to take a boat. She converses with all the mackerel and sharks she can find, although the whales are her favorite ones, because they are such good listeners. The shore is muddy once she reaches it, but she doesn't mind the rain so long as it doesn't mess up her new shoes. She carries her picnic basket across her back, which she unsaddles to take out fig jam and saltwater taffy.

Whenever she visits, my mother asks me when I plan to marry my lover. In that way, she is like every mother. She reminds me that she has to leave in the fall and I tell her it doesn't have to be like that. I wonder if she thinks a grandbaby will solve her loneliness, but I have already felt the darkness breathing on me. One more drowning mouth would extinguish our flame.

BROADSIDES & BOARDING PARTIES

No time for that stack of rules,
Intricate as rigging, nor the hassle
Of placing the wind on a compass,
Of finding depth or current,
The patience of the sea washed out

In our hunger for cannons, crashing
Masts, the crew's bodies slashed
Or peppered to pieces. We cranked up
Our ships for the crash, running
Through the powder and the cutlass.

In sixth grade we didn't wait for the pilot,
The cartographer. And maybe we still want
Blackbeard to drag us to his dark cabin, draw,
And blast us into daring, vital work.

AXIS & ALLIES

Washington has arranged his World War 2
game in the sun room, British planes
and German tanks await the rumble
of the dice, three days ago.

But again the sun goes down on the frozen
Soviet tundra, and Japan's ocean territory
holds its surface smooth as paper:
no one is left to witness another war,

Even if it turns out differently. Maybe
this go no one will stomp upstairs after
being reminded of a rule that foiled their plans,
or after the dice remind us of war's risk

And loss. The entire globe, laid down
amongst Jaime's geraniums and herblings,
sleeps soundly through another day; the long
shadows of the soldiers pace-out the equator.

FIRST LOVE: A CURRICULUM GUIDE

for Wichita, KS students, 1976-1981

1. Junior High

SEVENTH GRADE

HISTORY

To learn about the feudal system, perform skits. You, a tall, skinny girl with long tangly hair, will play the strapping serf Bartholomew. A scrawny, bony-elbowed boy we'll call Cole is cast as your son John. He wears wire-framed glasses and his lips look perpetually puckered.

You're beginning to see that junior high is itself a kind of feudal system, except instead of a hungry peasant serving the Lord and Lady of the manor, you're a low-pecking-order girl who has come to this junior high from a small elementary school out in the country. Your homemade T-shirts with ribbing around the collar and sleeves, the yoked tops your mother sews, the blue work shirt your cousin embroidered and that you were so proud of, all are all wrong, not to mention that you often have no idea what many of your classmates are talking about and wish a slang and curse word dictionary had been issued to get you up to speed.

So there you are, in front of the class, performing your skit, self-conscious, dressed all wrong, playing a serf named

Bartholomew. You tower over your son John, and everyone snickers.

ENGLISH

English class vocabulary lists accompany everything you read. *Deference, abyss, slake, hermaphrodite.* These are little use to you, not the words you really need definitions for, words that your classmates throw around, like, say, *virgin* or *gay.* Embarrassingly, you don't even know what these things are exactly. A virgin is someone unusually virtuous, good and upright, you guess, because church Christmas pageants and readings of the Christmas story always refer to Jesus's mother as the Virgin Mary. You have no clue what historical concepts of virtue entail.

You are shocked to learn from your elementary school friend Stacey that a virgin is actually someone who hasn't had sex, that there is a word for that. You have to ask Stacey what *gay* means, too. She has become more aloof, more concerned with being cool, since starting junior high. She says she is in love with an eighth grader. She stalks him in the halls. He leaves his shirt unbuttoned so that everyone can see the hair on his chest, and she reports to you every glance he casts her, every expression on his face, every word he speaks to her. You thought you knew what love meant, but this isn't it. And you don't know what to make of the fact that every word you don't understand seems to have something to do with sex.

ART

Your first assignment will be to draw something, anything, so that the teacher can assess your skills. Except your mind is blank. A girl at your table fleshes out a beach scene with playful dogs, bright-colored umbrellas, and guys in Speedos. Another outlines a circus clown and dumpy small elephants. You peel the paper off your crayon and sneak looks around the table. Kristie's people stretch out on lawn chairs in the sun, wearing dark sunglasses. Dana's elephant trunk curls around a peanut. She draws curves for the elephant's toenails and dark lines to suggest wrinkles.

Sweating profusely, desperate for an idea, you remember how, in sixth grade, you had to illustrate a scene from *A Wrinkle in Time*. You sketched a lumpy flying horse with Meg and Calvin balancing on its back. It was kind of a stupid picture, but you got into it, strokes loose and free as when you were about eight. You threw in stars and streaks of light. You drew the line at rainbows and unicorns, but the picture still looked like something sappy by a little kid. Except the teachers loved it. They passed it around and praised it.

So now all you can think to do is try to reproduce your flying horse picture. You don't have any time and you're too tense. Your drawing looks stiff and silly.

The teacher halts abruptly in front of you, squinting and tilting his head. He studies you, puzzled. His gaze travels back and forth between the picture and your face. He looks amused.

You burn with humiliation.

Things don't improve as the year goes on. While working on a pen and ink drawing of a sagging cracked boot, you accidentally smear the ink with the heel of your hand. While cutting out a mat for another drawing, your knife slips and leaves jagged edges. The teacher often throws up his hands at your sloppy work and questionable taste. He likes your rya rug design with somewhat phallic interlocking braids, but sighs when you choose red, pink, and white for it. Your room is pink, a color you have come to regret, and you think that a little red might toughen it up a little. It doesn't occur to you until later that your rug looks like a big Valentine.

HISTORY

You've never heard of Adolf Hitler until you find yourself in a small group trying to come up with a topic for a presentation. "I hate Hitler," says Cole, the boy with big lips who played your son John in the feudal system skit. "Let's do ours on Hitler."

You don't think Cole likes you, so you are extra nice to him, agreeing to his topic idea and laughing at his jokes about how stupid Hitler's mustache was. You are drawn to Cole, having seen him huddled in classroom doorways in the mornings, reading books, looking sad, and you laugh at his jokes during the history project and try to make him laugh in math class, where he sits across the aisle from you.

EIGHTH GRADE

MATH

When you first enter the math classroom, you automatically head toward Cole, but then you do a double take. He looks different; he has grown several inches and his lips fit him. He has grown into his lips. He is tall and tan with broad shoulders. His Izod shirt is skin-tight, outlining his swell of biceps. Suddenly intimidated, you duck into a chair two rows away and three seats behind him. He doesn't turn his head to say hi.

Examining him, you see that he's not quite as tall and

broad-shouldered as you thought, and his knit shirt is just too tight, not an Izod but a knockoff without a crocodile. His jeans have a worn sheen. Someone asks to borrow a pencil, and he smiles, braces glittering, and in that moment you see that he is your own weird scrawny sad Cole after all. But he still doesn't speak to you, and you regret that you didn't follow your first instinct and go sit beside him.

Then Stacey arrives, squealing: in the lunch line today, Paul said to her, "Can you hand me a fork?" She's pretty sure that means he likes her.

MATH, AGAIN

This is the only class you have with Cole, and you find yourself living from one math class to the next, hoping to have a chance to talk to him. You can't stop thinking about him, about how great he looks when he wears blue, about how sad he looks sitting in classroom doorways before school, poring over books: *Zen and the Art of Motorcycle Maintenance*, *The Screwtape Letters*, novels by Herman Hesse. You notice the key on a chain around his neck. You can't stop thinking about the day in the cafeteria that he leveled his gaze at you. How your eyes hooked and steadied and suddenly you were awash in inexplicable joy and deep tenderness and intense yearning.

And then, suddenly, in math, when he is only a few feet away and it's like all the little hairs on your arms are standing straight up, as if you are chilled by his very presence, you think, *I love Cole. I'm in love.*

You feel audacious. Brazen. Presumptuous. Like an imposter. How can this be love? When Stacey talks about love, about imagining running her fingers through Paul's tangle of chest hair, you think of fishy streams with hairy plants. When you think about Cole, it's like light glancing off a clear, cool spring.

ENGLISH

Your teacher reads the *Odyssey* out loud. You imagine yourself as Penelope, steadfast in your love, weaving and unweaving metaphorical shrouds. You will wait for him, your true love, for twenty years if necessary. You don't wonder if Odysseus, so easily distracted by Calypso and Circe, is worth it.

The teacher's voice fades. Her head droops. The wine-dark sea laps away into gentle snoring. You drift out of your daydream to a class full of students shifting and exchanging uneasy glances while the teacher breathes peacefully, dreaming.

MORE MATH

Math is effortless for Cole. People often scoot over beside him for help, and you wish you had the courage to do that, too, but you're good enough at math that he'd probably see right through it. "I hate gym," you hear him tell someone, and your heart swells with love, because you hate gym, too.

Sometimes you suspect that you are like a schizophrenic who believes that every swirl of wood grain is a secret message you must decode, every whisper of wind through trees a voice conveying profound truths only you can hear, the raised veins of a leaf a Braille fraught with meaning. You think of pioneer stories in which the gift of a candy cane or a penny in the toe of a stocking is a big deal. For you, even the most meager glance or words are treasures, things to savor. Even the smallest facial expression, word, gesture, or article of clothing feels like a veiled signal to you.

Ninth Grade
Math

Cole is not in your class.

English

Cole is not there either.

Music

It's girls' choir, but Cole isn't in the men's choir that meets next door at the same time, either. (That's what they call them at your school: girls and men.)

Gym

No Cole.

You bide your time. Plan paths from one class to another to maximize your chances of running into him. Years later, you can't remember a single thing you learned in ninth grade, only the perpetual distraction of looking for Cole everywhere, wondering, sometimes, if he actually existed or if you just made him up.

2. High School

Sophomore Year
Gym

You and Cole are in the same class, taught by a young, doe-eyed teacher, and an amazing thing happens. On the first day, just like that, as if you haven't been agonizing and plotting over how to get him to do this very thing, he comes over the first day and sits by you, all casual, like it's no big deal. It is true that neither of you knows anyone else in the class, but still, the moment that he plops down beside you on the bleachers seems fated. After that, you always sit together, you in your blue-and-white striped T-shirt and blue polyester shorts, Cole in his white undershirt and khaki shorts, and if you can still like each other in these unflattering outfits, it must be true love.

You're partners for tennis and archery. Every time you have to say the word "love" when announcing the tennis score, you feel your face blotch like a pink doily. You admire the sure flight of Cole's arrows next to the inebriated drift of their lazy companions shot by a row of classmates. Your own arrows tend to fall off the bow and plunk to the ground.

Waiting for your turn for tennis courts and the archery line, Cole tells you about his sister and his mother and his church and how he wants to be an Episcopal priest. When he says this, he quickly amends it: "Episcopal priests can get married." He wants to marry you, you think, feeling your life fall into place.

Often while he talks, all other sounds fade: balls bouncing on pavement and smacking against rackets, traffic passing on the nearby street. You collect details about Cole. How he writes his 7s the European way, bisected by a line. How he says, "How bourgeois," when classmates talk about their cars and their weekend parties. How he says "I-ther" instead of "Eether," and when he mentions boys who harass him at the bus stop he pronounces it "harris." How he likes a TV show called "Bosom Buddies" and has a German shepherd named Tequila and broke his arm when he was a kid, showing you the long scar, pink and shiny. How when he sneezes, you bless him in Spanish and he thanks you in German.

You listen to Cole talk and you peel apart grass blades,

reducing them to threads and tying the threads in knots. With your thumbnail, you slit open the stems of dandelions, studying their milky innards. This is how you feel when you are with him: slit open, insides showing, pulled apart, tied in knots.

JOURNALISM

You love this class, but the last fifteen minutes you're always distracted, watching the second hand on the wall clock, focused only on the moment when the tone will sound and you fly out of your chair and down the hall, feeling like the embodiment of every patient, abiding woman in fairy tales, epic poems, and proverbs. You are Cinderella, about to be whisked away by the prince after years of drudgery. You are Penelope, who'd woven and unwoven that shroud for twenty years before her faithfulness found its reward. You are on your way to being the noble wife worth more than rubies, whose husband and children will rise and call you blessed.

Every day, Cole waits for you under a tree in dapples of sunlight, foil-wrapped bologna sandwich and apple spread out on the grass. When you arrive from buying your daily cheeseburger and fries in a white paper bag from a small, nameless joint across the street, he asks, "What took you so long?"

"I didn't take that long," you always answer.

SPANISH

Te quiero mucho, you learn to say in Spanish, because your teacher insists that's how to say "I love you." Since she is always wandering from her lessons to rant about the immorality of abortion and since *te quiero mucho* seems to you to actually translate to "I like you very much," you're suspicious. Is teaching you to say only "I like you" part of her militant campaign against teen romance that might lead to pregnancy that might lead to abortion? She is doing her part to prevent this, you're convinced, by only permitting you to declare friendly affection, not passion. You look it up. *Querer*, you see, can also mean want, and since your yearning for Cole feels infinite, now you're really not sure what your teacher is up to.

GEOMETRY

In the margins of your notes, you scrawl your own proofs of Cole's love.

> *When I come to lunch every day, he asks what took me so long*
> *When it rarely takes more than ten minutes*
> *Which wouldn't seem so long if he weren't dying to see me*
> *So he must love me.*

BIOLOGY

Your scores soar during the genetics unit as you plot out the traits of your future children with Cole. High probability of brown eyes. Tall. Sensitive. Thoughtful. Attached earlobes. Straight hair. No dimples. Tongue rolling possible. Right-handed likely.

But you're on edge, because Cole seems perfectly happy to see you only at school. Some of your friends have started going to Friday night football games, but Cole declines to come. And not just that: he refuses invitations to make pizza at Kent's, to go to see *The Producers* at the Marple Theater and stop by Julie's afterward for cookies, to go roller skating on Saturday night with the group of quirky friends who sit with the two of you at lunch. Why doesn't he want to spend more time with you? How will you get married and have brown-eyed, dark-haired children at this rate?

Gym

You've always hated gym, but suddenly, it's the best part of the day, along with lunch and passing periods, walking through the halls together though you've never kissed, never held hands. Cole refuses invitations to social events, but once during passing period he agrees that after school he will go along on an excursion to a holography exhibit. Standing behind you, he moors his hands on your shoulders in a very boyfriend-like way, so why won't he come to weekend parties, and why won't he hold your hand? At Christmas during passing period, he pulls a wrapped gift from his locker: a sweetheart locket, gold carved with flowers and leaves and curling vines. Your breath catches: doesn't this mean he loves you?

In lulls between games and quizzes in gym class, you mention that maybe you'll become an Episcopalian, and Cole invites you to his church. He says he wants four kids someday, and you say you do, too, and you agree that you like the idea of Biblical names. Still, you never hold hands. You secretly wonder if you are repulsive.

"Why don't you kiss her?" a boy asks tauntingly in the hall, and Cole slams his fist against a locker. "You don't know how hard things are for me," he tells you, and you are touched at how shy he is, how lacking in confidence.

Junior Year

Algebra 2

You are always jiggling your foot, jiggling whole rows of chairs; you have too much pent up energy to sit still. One day, Cole, sitting in front of you, abruptly reaches out and grabs your foot, stopping it, and the whole class bursts out laughing at this uncharacteristic gesture, a simultaneous show of irritation and affection. "What's wrong?" he asks you one Friday when you are moping during class, and so you pass him a note: why won't he ever agree to go out on weekends? After that he finally, if often grudgingly, starts accepting invitations to go roller skating or come over with a group to watch *The Robe* on TV. You graduate to eating hard shell tacos on Friday nights while spinning around in plastic seats at Taco Tico, just the two of you, then go next door to the movie theater to see old movies like *Fiddler on the Roof* and *Jaws*. But you still never hold hands. He never puts his arm around you.

"Everyone holds hands," you finally say at the end of algebra, feeling inappropriately forward, positively brazen. "We should be original and just hold fingers." He laughs and agrees, and you do, hooking your little fingers together like a pinky swear, as he walks you to English. "My other fingers are feeling left out," you say at the end of the day, and by the next morning, you have advanced to whole-hand contact.

PSYCHOLOGY

You learn about B.F. Skinner and operant conditioning, how a pigeon can be taught to peck a lever ten times for each morsel of food, how then instead of releasing the food at fixed intervals, releasing it at variable ones can encourage the bird to keep on pecking the lever. By rewarding a behavior and then building on it, a mouse can be taught to run a maze, a dog can learn to drive, a child can be diverted from temper tantrums. Goals can be met by positively reinforcing each successive approximation toward that goal.

You break down your goal into steps. Talking, spending time together, holding hands: you've reached these goals. Next: first kiss, planning for the future, marriage. If you reward Cole for each small approximation toward that goal, you'll get there.

It never occurs to you that maybe it's he who is conditioning you, rewarding you at variable intervals, just enough to keep you hanging on.

AMERICAN HISTORY

Waiting for your first kiss proves excruciating. After movies you sit in your driveway in the Dodge Dart that Cole has borrowed from his mom, staring at each other and hinting around. "I hope your parents don't think we're doing anything immoral out here," Cole says, or "I wish I had more confidence. I wish I wasn't so shy. I wish I was normal." You finally slide out of the car, cross the dark to the porch where flying bugs congregate around the light, hear his car back out to the street, slowly, slowly, idling, a crunch of gravel, a rush backward, a puff of air. Will your hopes always disappear in a puff of air? You don't know whether to laugh or cry.

And then, finally, at the duck pond one night, you throw bread to the birds, who pluck it out of the air and snatch it out of the water. You talk and tear off pieces and throw them. You are so absorbed in the conversation, you're surprised to see that the bloated ducks have all drifted away and that the water's surface is thick with soaked bread, a layer of mushy pond scum. And you both laugh and then, because Cole is wearing a button that says "Kiss me, I speak German," you finally kiss him. It leaves your lips soft.

You kiss and kiss that night, and he says in wonder, "We're together. We're finally together," as if he, too, has been waiting and doubting. He tells you that he used to plan his suicide, and you are touched that he was ever so sad.

Now you sit close together during a class film. While a booming voice describes the pre-World War II climate in Europe, Cole reaches for your hand. Slowly, his index finger traces up your arm and down again, elbow to wrist, wrist to elbow. Shivers follow the path of his finger. It slips under your sleeves, toward forbidden territory under clothes. It brushes the white undersides of your upper arms, circles up to your bra strap, slides back to the crook of your arm.

Blood rushes to your face as your skin tingles with small glorious shocks. You lay your arm on his desk and settle your shoulder against his. The length of his arm presses against the length of yours.

Dust swims in the projector's fan of light. Occasionally, someone shifts, the curve of a shoulder or globe of a head nicking the corner of the film. Light and shadow jerk and jump onscreen, across Cole's face. His fingertips circle the bones of your wrist and map out branches of veins.

The film flicks off, and your ears ring in the sudden silence, your eyes dazzled by the shock of overhead lights. The projector's fan breathes quietly.

Everyone else shuffles and rustles and murmurs, but you can't move. Something you don't have a name for has just transformed you completely. If you try to grasp this joy and light and yearning, you suspect it will turn to liquid and run through your fingers.

"Let's go," Cole says to you, but all you can do is blink at him.

EXTRACURRICULARS

Cole is opposed to spirit week, pep rallies, football games or other athletic events, honor societies, clubs, or other school activities. He is opposed to anything that smacks of groupthink. Years later, when friends reminisce about proms and parties, you draw a blank.

You will remember being completely happy, though, seeing Cole all day at school. Once it turns cold out, you eat together with friends in front of a bank of lockers in D hall, talk to him on the phone each night, make out on a couch in his basement on Friday nights. His basement is unfinished, the couch mildewed, the bumpy walls water-streaked, his childhood train set spread out on a table complete with tiny fir trees and a post office. He puts clothes in the washer to drown out noise as you peel off each other's shirts and kiss on the couch with creaky springs. The spin cycle bumps to a stop. You hear the soft spray of water that introduces the rinse cycle. You offer him the daisy from your bra, and he is scandalized.

This would all be perfect if Cole weren't less interested in making out than you are, if he didn't often plead exhaustion, a stomachache, a sinus headache. You attribute his pulling away to a difficult and distracting home life. His father died when he was just five and his mother, whom you've met only in passing, who is pale, soft-spoken, and angular, the bones in her face prominent, without softness, haunts the house like a ghost. He tells you that she struggles with emphysema and mental illness.

You and Cole are on course, planning your future, even choosing a wedding date after college graduation. But more and more, he says things like, "I don't know if I really want to be a priest," or "Maybe I'll become a monk" or "When I graduate, I'm going to an underdeveloped country in Africa to teach," as if the two of you haven't already figured out your lives, how you'll go to college together, then move to New York City and put him through seminary by working for a magazine. There are days when Cole's mysterious sadness looms fierce and impenetrable next to your small, childish sorrows, and you don't know how to get through to him.

But then it's summer and you ride your moped to his house, the moped your dad got you so you could take summer classes at the university. You and Cole ride around together, pretending to be tough-talking chain-smoking bad kids, sophisticated and European, not two honors students on a motorbike that only goes 30 mph. Cole tells you all about *The Confessions of St. Augustine* and religious holidays that you don't know about, like All Saints Day. But in the midst of this, he says more and more things like, "I wish I had a normal family." "What's normal?" you answer. "I wish I were normal," he goes on. "I wish I had a normal life." You agree that you wish his family was more stable, but you've always felt abnormal yourself. Why can't you be abnormal together?

"You don't get it, you can't get it," he says mournfully.

Senior Year
Study Hall

"It concerns me to see a student of your caliber taking study hall," says the guidance counselor. You look at him blankly.

You and Cole are taking study hall together so that your English and humanities classes will align also. You have almost all the credits you need for graduation but would never consider finishing early because you want to be with Cole.

But he is increasingly moody. He doesn't talk about it much, but you know that his mother has to be hospitalized regularly. Who wouldn't be anguished sometimes, given such circumstances? You feel like a silly, superficial child when he becomes distant, desperate to understand him, but he shuts you out and refuses to talk about it. Once his mother goes into the hospital and he doesn't even tell you about it until the next week.

And then one night, on the phone, he starts to cry. He says he can't continue with this relationship. This makes no sense to you. After years of murkiness and uncertainty, the two of you have now been inseparable for two years, your life locked into a lucid picture like all the pieces of a jigsaw finally in place. How can he possibly disassemble all of this in just one night, one conversation? You don't believe him. He will come around, you think.

But in study hall the next day, he gives you a note.

Sometimes I doubt my sexuality, he has written.

You wonder what that means. That he doesn't have any?

He asks you to return the note so that he can burn it. It is years before you understand that he might have been afraid of more than exposure or ridicule. That maybe he was afraid for his life.

ENGLISH

During every quarter, you have chosen a module of

novels to read, broadening your knowledge of Jewish writers, naturalists, and the Romantic Period. You loved Malamud, Potok, Hardy, Dreiser. You read *Wuthering Heights* and went around thinking, *I am Cole, he's always, always in my mind, not as a pleasure any more than I am always a pleasure to myself, but as my own being.* You read "Annabel Lee" and went around thinking, *my darling, my darling, my life and my bride.*

Now, you can't concentrate. You're supposed to be finishing the romance module, but you can't bear to think about romance when Cole is avoiding you despite the dark circles under his eyes that suggest that he is miserable without you. You try to talk to him in study hall. "I'm not happy, and you're not happy," you say.

"I'm not happy," he acknowledges, and for the briefest second, hope flickers. Then he adds, "But I'm content."

You stay planted there before him, trying to process this, wondering how he has become such a stranger.

"Someone has to walk away," he tells you, impatiently. So you turn abruptly and leave, weaving between tables in the cafeteria, confused. After that you often spend study hall driving around town in the used car your dad just bought to replace your moped. You don't eat, don't sleep, and neither, it appears, does Cole, but his mind is firmly made up.

When you try to go back to the romance module, you can't concentrate. Most of these books don't seem romantic to you at all, just boring.

On the last day of school, your English final question is, "What does the arrow represent in Robert Louis Stevenson's *The Black Arrow*?" You panic. You never got past the book's first page.

The seat in front of you, where Cole used to sit, is empty. He has been skipping classes. He even skipped the AP exam.

You try to concentrate. On the word *black*, on the word *arrow*. Black: like the last few months, feeling your way through darkness, the light on which you based your life suddenly erased. Arrow: you remember the confident flight of Cole's arrows during the gym class archery unit, how they soared like Type A birds bulleting south. How others' arrows wobbled and turned in flight, missing the target, how your own never quite rose into flight at all. It all seems like an omen, looking back, his sure sense of direction contrasted against your own waffling inability to make a future without him.

But you can't write any of this in an essay that's supposed to be about Robert Louis Stevenson.

Then the fire drill bell starts clanging, reverberating off the walls, and you put down your pen in relief and, with your classmates, scatter into the hall. "Has anyone read *The Black Arrow*?" you ask, whispering up and down the line, until you run into another girl doing the same thing, except she's asking, "Has anyone read *Anna Karenina*?"

You end up outside on the steps summarizing the plot of *Anna Karenina*, an act that earns you enough good karma that on your way back into the classroom, someone sidles up to you and says, "*The Black Arrow* is kind of a retelling of *Robin Hood*."

Back inside, you write, "In *The Black Arrow*, a retelling of *Robin Hood*, the black arrow is both symbolic and literal. There is a real arrow, which is black, that is an important device in taking from the rich and giving to the poor. It is also symbolic."

You know that you'll fool no one, but you go on writing. Later, you won't remember anything that you actually wrote, only that in that half hour you crossed the threshold beyond restraint into total abandon, because in the long run, what did anything matter anyway? Maybe you wrote about how some arrows fly in straight paths to their targets. How others flounder. Maybe you worked in the phrase "slings and arrows of outrageous fortune." Maybe you wrote about the expression "straight arrow" and about stabbing others in the back with arrows. Maybe you pondered the origin of the word "quiver." Years later, mostly what you'll remember is that feeling that came over you, of being immersed in something bigger than yourself, writing, writing, until you got to the last line, wrapping it up: "And so, in *The Black Arrow*, it is significant that the arrow is black, which reinforces the symbolism in this retelling of the *Robin Hood* story."

ECONOMICS

You didn't study for the economics final, either. The first question asks you to explain the difference between causation and correlation and to give illustrations.

You're stumped. But then you remember how you felt earlier that day when you wrote your English essay, so you pick up your pen and get started, at first haltingly, then flowingly. Writing carries you back to that day in the sixth grade, before you'd ever met Cole, when you felt loose and free, drawing a picture of Meg and Calvin flying through the sky on a horse. You were so absorbed in your drawing that it hadn't mattered what anyone thought. You just drew and drew and felt more like yourself than ever before.

And so now you write whatever comes into your head until you imagine throwing in stars and streaks of light and rainbows and unicorns. It is soothing, this mishmash of thoughts and images that appear on the page, writing that won't make sense to anyone else but somehow brings you back to yourself, writing that you will remember fragments of even years later.

If you break up with your boyfriend after eating a peach, you write, you might conclude that the peach caused the breakup, when actually the peach is just correlated with the breakup, which was caused by a million factors you will never understand. Maybe there's something wrong with you. Or maybe his mother is sick, maybe he feels burdened by responsibility. Maybe none of that has a single thing to do with the peach. Maybe daring to eat a peach really does disturb the universe. You read "Prufrock" in your college class last summer, and you're especially proud of that line. You're so proud of that line, you briefly forget your misery.

The last question asks for an example of a monopoly. You dash off one last line and turn in your test.

"God has a monopoly on butterflies," you have scribbled, and it seems like the most profound thing you've ever written.

GRADUATION

You and Cole march in together to *Pomp and Circumstance* because after your breakup, it was too late to change partners. You curse the mortarboards that make everyone look even more unattractive than gym uniforms do. But it probably wouldn't matter. Cole makes vague polite conversation with you, then keeps drifting away to talk animatedly to another boy. They keep cracking up.

After graduation, you go home, not to any parties. You try to remember anything you learned in school beyond a few

Spanish words and phrases, how to write a geometry proof, scattered facts about the feudal system and the Industrial Revolution, the concept of operant conditioning, which seems to work better on birds than on people. Vocabulary words like *deference, abyss, slake, hermaphrodite.*

You think of all of the words you still don't fully understand, the kinds of words that only take on meaning from experience, like *sex*, or *love*, or *gay*. You have fallen into an abyss. Into a thirst that can never be slaked. You wonder if you will ever understand.

CEDAR WAXWINGS

Six soft birds ruffled by wind lie silent on the walk.
   We do not talk, those who have circled around
      the strange congregation to hold them in our hands

like feathered prayers. The bodies tremor, almost dead
   from flying into windows where the sky dared each bird,
      as if driven by its name, to turn Icarus gone too close to the sun.

The plumed shapes crashing against
   the invisible plain of glass, some mystery
      the feathered body cannot pass. They must

have seen themselves rushing headlong
   at themselves before an awful ecstasy
      quivered through them like the crush of bone,

the body now a stone in which
   the slowed heart rests, the unwinding
      muscle of the breath a whistled tomb.

Their bodies bloom blood
   onto the walk. We scoop them
      into bags, do not talk about the down

sticking to our fingers, stuccoed
    to the ground, our how when we drop
        them in the bin, the hollow thump sounds like sin.

RESIDENT MERLIN

You came swooping through
like a silver bullet train
dipping under the porch roof
strafing the feeders.
That first time we followed your
flightpath back to a thick cluster
of glossy leaves and branches
in the tall maple just over the back fence.

The finches and chickadees
had instantly vanished.
All birdsong ceased as suddenly
as if someone had dropped night's cover
over the day.

Then after a while we lost you,
assumed you'd moved on to other
hunting grounds, and eventually
they returned — the finches, the chickadees,
the wrens and nuthatches,
all ravenous, jockeying for seed.

I love that a group of you may be
an "illusion" —

and I thought maybe that was what *you* were
in all your singularity.

But now here you come
again, blasting through!
And the dead air
in your wake . . .

So you've moved into the
neighborhood, have you? Taken up
residence
in the greenway
behind our house?

Splendid creature,
doing what falcons do . . .

POWERS AND AUTHORITIES

We helped clear the garage after Aunt Bridget sent Grampa to the home, stacking old snow tires by the curb, using the nearly empty cans of Rust-oleum to make squiggles on the cement stairs. The jelly jars of antique nuts and bolts, the rusting Yuban coffee cans of bent nails, could be marketed on Ebay, but Uncle Jimmy said, Fuck it, trash it, each and every screw - we have no time to sort through his bullshit. Uncle Jimmy wanted the snow shovels though, and when he took them from the wall, something odd was left on the plaster, a stained figure all cobwebby — an angel — only the head and wings and strange misshapen feet.

Aunt Bridget made us lunch. Grilled cheese sandwiches and tomato soup. Sides of green piccalilli and pale glasses of Miller High Life. For the young ones, juice squeezed from the concord grapes tangled over the backyard arbor. Aunt Bridget laid the sandwiches on the table, sandwiches formed in the shape of angels — two brown toasted wings and a golden head of cheddar.

"I got used to it with your Grampa. Angel this, Angel that."

In front of us, Uncle Jimmy bit the cheesy head off one. Not scarily, no, not at all.

That was the day Aunt Bridget said our family was blessed to have such good looking grandchildren.

Grampa lasted a week in the facility. One morning the attendants found him stiff and cold and dead at the bottom of the long gravel driveway, the knees of his pajama bottoms ripped bloody. He had been trying to crawl onto VFW Parkway to home. After the Mass, some of us arrived early to the cemetery, waiting beside Granma's grave, Uncle Jimmy leaning against the headstone sucking on a Marlboro Red. Yet the silvery hearse just rolled on past, in the limo Aunt Bridget by herself sitting upright. The two vehicles glided all the way to the wrought iron fence where unexpectedly a deep hole had already been dug, a man's grave beside a damp marble slab level with the yellowed grass. The stone said, and this was all it said, "ANGELINA."

ASHLEY STIMPSON

HEAVY-HANDED SYMBOLISM IN AN INDIANA POST OFFICE

I mail my divorce papers
signed hastily —
notarized by a stranger —
from the old post office in Richmond, Indiana
home of the Red Devils.
As I force all that paper-clipped disappointment
a slow reckoning of my failures
(I always loved words)
into a rigid envelope rejecting it
a woman enters moaning.
Lunch-breakers and court-runners, stay-at-home mothers
turn toward her trembling.
She has run over a cat and unknowingly
dragged it for miles
alive.

It is breathing, just barely.
She needs someone to deliver that last, brutal blow.

I laugh —
that sardonic laugh that made you irate —
and with violent fingers somehow seal
this quiet batch of misery.

ASHLEY STIMPSON

CHANGING MY NAME AT THE PROBATE COURT

The fourth time it was really over
A man with a hand-held voice recorder
And ill-fitting shirt sleeves
Gave me back my name.

He sent me out into a heat wave
Of hungry reporters
Waiting on a death-row conviction

A tribe of red-haired children —
Weeping because visiting hours had ended —
Herded by an ample woman
Holding the youngest one wailing
Into the folds of her glistening neck

A discarded tomcat beneath my car begging
Never mind that the meter was up.

And in this cacophony of tragedies
I couldn't help
But hear my own,
The loudest
The most exquisite of them all.

SNAG PINE

The particles of my mother and father's love settled like the cracks
in the ceiling tucked in a place most will never notice and now
the floor creaks phantom yells I pray won't wake the baby.

Pots and pans are not the same since my mother used them
to make bruises on her arms and chest but still I brown our
    meat in the skillet
and put the stew on to simmer for hours while my father sits
    and smokes.

He talks about suicide daily but not because she's gone or
    because regret.
I don't know what the steam from the pot is telling me or the dust
that sleeps on our smiling portraits. Who was it behind the lens?

The dead pine towering above is stiff with twisted, leafless
    branches
as trees around it breathe and sway. The room darkens as a
    storm moves in,
and I think of the things we'll miss when she falls.

METAPHYSICAL SIBLINGS

Upon learning that my brother, who isn't
me, reached the summit of Mount Rainer,
a summit I'll never reach, I try to

take stock of the situation. I want to stop
thinking of conjunction, because a valley
isn't a cavity in the earth, which makes

complete, unclear sense. I want to
do only what I can do, which is to distinguish
a world from the world in me. In me, who is

taller than my brother, a snow-capped hill
is Mount Rainer, or isn't until I undertake
the short, credibly invigorating climb.

GOLGOTHA

As sacred as the sites I learned from scripture,
I too saw our hill as a place of crucifixion,
as an empty lot that bore the slow-death
of every season: football, winter, baseball, spring,
month after month of double-plays and Hail Mary's,
of passes, pitches, aluminum bats and pigskins
that when the neighborhood boys and I grew
tired of, we swapped for our marble collections.
Though ready to repeat the shit-talk we were so new
at inflecting, we kept silent as we formed a circle,
dropped marbles at our feet, and as some boys —
as though bordering on parody — performed the stations
of the cross, prepared themselves with the idea
that God took sides and would take theirs if they took
the game more seriously. And how could they not?
How could we look on and toss marbles from our bags
without thinking of sacrifice? Without realizing
that more than one of us would come away
empty-handed, that after the click, clack, and click
of glass against glass, after winning pieces
that looked like bumblebees, beach balls, onion skin,
oxblood, cat's and devil's eyes, tiger stripes
and toothpaste, we'd lose track of time, and lose
another day that brought us to where we stood;

that mound of dirt where we poured ourselves
for hours into each shot, and where I'd stop
to watch the sun melt above the unfinished frames
of houses, aware, only years later, of how dusk
bruised the chain-link, warped and wooden fences,
and of how our shadows — shriveled, thirsty —
pooled so quickly across that unanointed ground.

ALL WELCOME

Sun-laced snow glows through the stained glass image of John the Baptist wading in the waters. She should be thinking Christian thoughts but she's thinking of Eskimos. There's a different name they use now, it won't come to her, no matter. An Eskimo hunter in his sealskin parka, polar bear breeches with the warm fur against his skin, lying on the ice at a blowhole, harpoon poised for that fraction of an instant when the seal comes up for air. Waiting, waiting, waiting, then wham! Blood in the water, blood on the ice, drive the harpoon in deep enough to hold while he hacks and hacks with his bone knife to widen the blowhole, to hold when he drags a mass of meat and skin and blubber up onto the ice and onto the sled to be pulled home in triumph by the yelping voracious dogs who will get a share just like everyone else.

Everyone gets a share. Seal eyeballs popped into the mouths of children, flesh boiled over a lamp of seal oil, bones for sleds and needles, gut for snowshoes and sled traces, precious skin for warmth. Nothing wasted, nothing wasted. In her pew she sighs over waste. Half-eaten sandwiches her niece leaves on the plate. Not her fault, a child shouldn't eat more than she wants, but doesn't her mother realize? Just give her half a sandwich, more if she asks. But that's too much trouble, easier to make it all at once and throw it away. Or eat it yourself so it doesn't go to waste, no wonder her sister has gained so much weight.

That's wasteful too, isn't it, to eat what you don't need?

She should be paying attention to the service. The minister seems like a nice enough man. Our Father who art in Heaven. That's where her own father is, presumably. He collected only an average-sized catalog of sins in his average-length life, nothing dreadful enough to keep him out of Heaven, if there is such a place. Dying itself can't be held against him. He didn't do it on purpose, seemed to try pretty hard not to do it, period. It's been a bad year, that's all.

Blowing snow. That's why the congregation is small this morning, too hard to get up on the weekend to shovel yourself out. And why she's thinking of Eskimos in their ice houses, stripped naked to keep from overheating. An oil lamp and a crowd of bodies, not warm enough to melt the roof but too hot for furs and pelts. Perpetual darkness till it's perpetual light. How does the body stretch its rhythms? Wake and sleep, sleep and sleep again, but there's always hunger to contend with. No one hunts in a blizzard, you couldn't see the tail of the first dog, nothing to do but sleep and hope the seal meat from the last hunt holds out and the storm doesn't drive off every living thing so even if you survive the storm you starve anyway.

She's never been that kind of hungry. Every person in this prosperous church has had a nice breakfast unless they didn't feel like eating and just grabbed a cup of coffee to warm their insides against winter. Life-and-death hunger, that's not part of her world, it's only something to imagine and why would she want to imagine that? Eskimo infants crying when the teat runs dry because the blizzard goes on not for two days but eight and there's been nothing to eat for six of those days because the last hunt failed and there you are in the ice house with your

111

husband the failed hunter and your furtive mother-in-law and the listless three-year-old and the squalling starving infant. When do you give up and put him out in the storm? And when do you stop listening for the difference between the shriek of the storm and the shriek of the baby you're murdering for its own sake? You can still hear him, your own, your treasured child. And why is she thinking of these things here in church where her thoughts should be of God? The same God who starves the babies, who commands the seal to pour its blood on the pristine ice. The God who creates divorce and causes jobs of thirteen years to disappear with one week's notice and thirteen weeks' severance pay.

John the Baptist wading in the waters. The Holy Land, where snow rarely falls. It's the heat there, drought, water's the jewel, not seal meat. The minister is giving a sermon on forgiveness, on welcoming, judge not lest ye. Different church, different minister, though it meant driving further on a snowy Sunday, anything better than the heartfelt sympathy of people she knows. Everyone here looks up blankly cheerful at the plump earnest man who's trying hard to waken their spiritual feelings, never letting on if they agree with him or just politely let him talk. Open your hearts to your fellow man. She wonders where her heart might be located. That spot in her chest isn't icy, just cool. Not arctic, just north temperate. Has her heart adapted to her climate? Is that why her husband finally gave up and took a job in Massachusetts? Does the Eskimo mother feel cold-hearted about her freezing infant? Does she weep?

No way to know. Childless, she has no way to feel it inside. Can you only know in others what you've experienced yourself? Then why does arctic cold feel native? Snow glitters and whirls outside an abidingly pious John the Baptist. The sun glints through his halo, through windy spinning snow, casts vague shadows that don't quite light on the other worshippers. Each with his own thoughts, or hers, always more women than men. The skull is such a fortress, the eyes are windows, the mouth a door, but how do you know whether it's the truth that walks out? He said there was no other woman, but what if he just plain lied? And even if it's her own door and she truly wants to send truth out into the world, it turns out she can't really command truth no matter how hard she tries, and no one can receive it anyway because they always sift it through the sieve of what they're already sure of.

Snow. The Eskimo hunter lying for hours on the ice, staring at the blowhole, waiting. Each seal has several blowholes and you never know which one it will use or how long it will stay under water without needing air at all. So you have to be poised and ready while nothing happens. Nothing happens. Over and over again nothing happens. But then suddenly it does and if you're too slow or you've been dreaming of seal meat or of the beauties of your wife or of the last time you drove your harpoon in vicious and triumphant with blood swirling in the waters, if your unreliable mind is rambling off somewhere else then the seal blows and disappears while the poised harpoon hangs idiotically in mid-air. Then you have to wait all over again, hoping the seal doesn't abandon that blowhole completely. Or else you give up and your infant son starves and the rest of your family eventually dies along with him. Will it be your mother or your three-year-old to go first?

Lying on the ice in the motionless solitude. Is there any bit of daylight, does the sun leak just a little pink across the blank ice? Or is it just dark, no way to distinguish the hours unless you can read the wheel of stars. Endless stars, moonless day, not a sound except the ice shattering and groaning under the unthinkable weight of cold. And you have no choice but to lie there just as frozen, as if you were ice with a heartbeat, still a few thoughts turning slowly inside your head, still the capacity to know the ache in that upraised arm that you don't dare lower because any instant could be the instant, there's nothing to do but wait. And because there's no daylight there's no time, only the stars whispering to each other things you're not allowed to know in a language you can't hear.

Or it's light, perpetual day. Still you lie on the ice, your life devoted to lying on the ice. Sunlight glaring across the violent jumbled ice, waters thrown up and stuck there, looming shapes natural to your eyes so accustomed to the heartless ways of cold. You know it isn't cruelty because there's no intent, only mindless cold mindlessly being itself. You lie on the ice, the only half-dark shape in a wilderness of white, sky white, ice white, crags and boulders of snow glazed white and white to their very hearts though snow has no heart. Everything is motionless. You are motionless, the light is motionless, time is motionless, and within this motionlessness your particular self slowly evaporates and disappears. Your skull fails to protect your mind. Your individual consciousness gradually seeps out and you become another frozen block in the frozen landscape. You can still hear your pulse in your ears but your skin and flesh grow misty. You are no longer lying on ice, you are floating on ice, in ice, in whiteness. Though your harpoon arm is still raised there is no longer arm or harpoon or blowhole or anything else. There is no longer up or down, sky or land.

There is only whiteness, whether you turn or roll or curl or cry out, there is only whiteness. You are swallowed up in whiteness and you cannot even think to stand because within whiteness there is no ground, there is no sun above and ice below, it is all one and you are within that one and you will float within whiteness through all eternity.

So when the seal blows and gasps just inches from your face you can only stare at him, his eye gazing into yours, his eternity matching your own, your arm no more able to strike than your brain to grasp what isn't white. You're no longer a hunter, you're just another incarnation of limitless whiteness and the seal knows. He pauses, puffing the lymph of fishes into your nostrils, seeing you with not pity but clear-eyed recognition, taking his slow time to fill his lungs before plunging down out of sight. And then you gather yourself and stand, not because you believe there is anything to stand on, only because your body long ago mastered the mechanics of standing. The surviving animal inside you makes you stagger back to your empty sled so your dogs can carry you back to your ice house where your wife looks at your ice-blank face and sees the whiteness in your eyes and knows in that moment that either she hunts or you're all doomed.

The last hymn. She is standing and singing with everyone else, the long-memorized animal mechanics of singing. All welcome, Saint John with his halo prepared to baptize her with all the others who believe or hope or wish or pray to believe, belief would be so much easier, there would be ground under her feet and real human faces to greet, not a sea of whiteness at which she smiles the best she can.

HUSH

Midnight feedings — shards of glass
slide through my nipples.
His constant cries shatter
like crashing rows of snow globes —
broken glass, water, small worlds.
The idyllic lullabies crack
with what mama couldn't buy.
My body — tattered and bloated,
stranded in bed — couldn't scratch
a path to my secondhand sanctuary —
that old rocking chair —
off-white fabric sagging into gray,
consecrated by the common stains
of other mothers and children.
If I could fingernail my way
down the hall,
climb into its cushions,
it could sooth me,
coo me into motherhood.
Its mockingbird song
echoing through the night.

THE ROMANTIC ERA

Before Alex Rook got married and had children, before his wife opened up a bed and breakfast and perhaps had an affair, before customers complained that the B&B was haunted — before Alex's life fell apart — he was 22 and sitting on the hood of his car in an empty liquor store parking lot, holding the envelope that contained the answer to his marriage proposal.

The proposal, such as it was, took place two weeks before on a shaded walking path which traversed the Michigan State campus. It was raining softly at first as Alex walked with Susan, which he considered a good sign. Then it stopped raining and Alex considered this a good sign too, but it got colder, a breeze turned surly, birds sought cover, and he gave up looking for signs. He moved in front of Susan and showed her the engagement ring. She was silent.

"Susan?"

Alex looked down at the ring in his outstretched hand, wondering if it looked like something else to Susan. Two students approached, one after the other, walking toward him; he waited until both had passed before speaking again. "It's an engagement ring," he said.

She nodded.

"Susan . . ." Alex prayed for her to say something. Something affirmative.

"O.K, so . . ." He spoke to the ground in between them.

"Think of all the time we've spent together. We could keep doing that. That's why people get married. And we . . . we've got chemistry. What more do you need?"

Silence.

"We're like two peas in a pod."

Susan finally spoke: "What?"

Alex looked at her. "I mean, we're similar," he said. "We mesh."

"How many peas are in a pod?"

"What?"

"Nothing. It doesn't matter."

"But it does matter!" Alex closed up the ring in his outstretched hand and, with some hesitation, brought it back to his side. "I mean, best friends should get married whenever possible. That's what people say. Married people say it."

Silence.

Alex looked around, wondering why every student hadn't stopped what they were doing to listen in on this conversation, then thinking that maybe they were. "I have to say I didn't expect this. I've accepted the job in Baltimore. Were you just going to let me leave?"

"What do you mean?"

"Are you seeing someone else?"

"What?"

"Is that a yes?"

"No."

"No? Is that your answer?"

"Yes. No! I don't mean your proposal. I don't have an answer to that yet. I think I want to write it down."

Alex thought she meant right away. She clarified that it

would likely take her two weeks to respond.

"Two weeks?"

"Getting married is a big deal."

Alex stared at her, looking for a clue, but her eyes told him nothing. "Right. Two weeks. I'll have moved back home by then."

"So I should send it to your parents?"

"Yes. I mean, don't address it to them. Send it to me."

She asked him for that address, which she then wrote on a tissue she found in her purse.

They parted then, Susan giving Alex a quick hug. He stood still and watched her walk away, waiting for her to turn around, to say something, to come running back, to do something other than walk around a bend and disappear from sight. Alex remained in place for several minutes, wishing it would start to rain again, hard enough to drown him.

For the next six days Alex had little interest in eating or sleeping. Two days later he became an official 1985 graduate of Michigan State University; Susan still had a year to go. He then managed to eat and sleep himself into a state of feeble optimism while moving back in with his parents. Five more days passed until the letter arrived on a Saturday morning, but when it did Alex was unable to open it.

Susan and he had spoken almost every day for two years until the proposal, but since then not a word. They'd talked of college classes, movies, song lyrics, parents, sometimes of the future, and Susan did most of the talking. Philosophy was her favorite subject, and Alex her favorite listener. He liked to listen. They meshed like that, he thought.

"Only birds are at peace," she once said. "Every other creature longs for the ability to fly. Especially people. It makes them restless."

"But people can get in planes," Alex said.

"That only makes it worse, because then people can sense what they are missing."

Alex nodded his head, thinking that sounded right. He thought she was brilliant; she was flattered by his thought.

She once asked Alex, "Do you have a secret that you've never told anyone?"

He did. "I lost my mother's wedding ring and never told her."

"What were you doing with your mother's wedding ring?"

"Pretending to be Bilbo in *The Hobbit*. She was doing some work in the yard, and her ring was sitting on the kitchen table. I saw it there and put it on, then went back in the woods and pretended I was in Middle Earth. At some point it slipped off my finger but I didn't notice. My mother was really anxious when she couldn't find it. I knew that she didn't tell my dad it was lost while she looked for it every day. Eventually she got a new one."

Susan squinted her eyes. "So you're an invisible person."

"What?"

"Studies have shown that when people are asked what super power they would choose, they all choose either flight or invisibility. It's obvious now that you're one of the invisibles."

And Alex nodded his head, thinking this sounded right.

Alex recalled this conversation during the days that he waited for Susan's letter. Perhaps losing his mother's wedding ring was a sign that he would never marry, or should never marry, and wondered if Susan thought the same.

Then the letter arrived, and Alex decided he would open it only after leaving his parents' upstate Michigan home for Baltimore the next day. If she turned him down, he wanted to be in the middle of a journey, believing that somehow this would lessen his misery. He told his parents that he was leaving the next day to get a head start on his apartment search. They knew nothing of his marriage proposal, and if Susan turned him down then they were never to find out at all; they might take it personally. He still had some hope, but the chance that he would be going out into the world untethered and alone was gathering space in his mind.

And so on a Sunday morning in May, Alex packed his bags and the letter, and drove his car toward Baltimore and his future job there as a financial analyst. (The next day he remembered that he forgot to say goodbye to his parents.)

Late that evening Alex got off Highway 80, somewhere in Eastern Ohio, and began driving back roads. Years later he tried to remember whether he had gone looking for a liquor store or merely happened to find one. Whatever the case, the time had come. He would buy champagne and scotch, and then open the letter. If Susan agreed to marry him, he would open the champagne; if not, the scotch was in order. But it was Sunday night, and back then liquor stores were closed on Sundays. Alex was unaware of this. He drank beer and had only tasted whiskey once.

Alex got out of his car with the letter folded in his front pocket, thinking of it as a map of his future. He pulled it out and held it up in the simple moonlight. The time had come; he would take it sober. He turned his headlights on so he could read the letter, then sat up on the hood of his car, looking around, convinced that he would remember every detail of this place, the store's dark green awning and ad-filled windows, the white lines of the parking lot, the dark crooked lines of the trees by the side of the road, the bend in the road up ahead that led to Baltimore. He was alone in the parking lot, about to open the letter and receive the answer to his marriage proposal. Except he already knew the answer. She was turning him down.

He'd known all along, he admitted that to himself now. If he'd truly believed that there was a chance of Susan writing "I will marry you," he would have stayed around so he could drive to her home and celebrate with her in premarital bliss. What Susan did not want - what no woman wanted - was to accept her marriage proposal via the mail. She told him she would write a letter because it gave her time to find the right words and gently let him down, and it allowed her to be somewhere else when he found out she was breaking his heart; that was who she was. She was confident in most matters yet was unable to reject someone face-to-face. There in the parking lot he felt alone on a stage, and everyone he knew was in the audience, silent in the surrounding darkness, staring at him and shaking their heads, taking pity on him but thinking he should have known. He opened the letter, scanning it in case he was wrong. He wasn't.

The letter was three pages long, though he needed only a few seconds to discover that she had left him no reason to hope that she would change her mind. He drove in silence the rest of the night with the front windows rolled down, listening to the sound of distant cars, the letter face down on the passenger seat beside him.

"The Recovery"—as Alex later called it—began with a halfhearted suicide attempt that summer involving Nyquil in excess of the recommended dosage. He lost his appetite for about six months, and found Susan continually showing up in his dreams, though she was always silent and beyond reach.

A month after starting his new job Alex finally looked at Susan's letter again, and once he did he became obsessed with it. He read it aloud, he read it by candlelight, he analyzed it word by word. She wrote, "I'm a flight person, while you are obviously an invisible one. In the long run it would never work." One stupid story about pretending to be Bilbo Baggins turned him into a member of the other camp? Though he did consider himself one of the invisibles, if he had to choose between the two; he wanted to disappear altogether. "We discussed going our separate ways once you graduated . . ." Had they? He would have remembered. "We never discussed marriage . . ." No doubt about that. She also thought that his interpretation of the Talking Heads song "Burning Down the House" was too literal. "Yet another example of our differences," she wrote. Some evenings Alex did nothing but analyze the letter, looking for hope in its hidden meanings. He doubted Susan was unhappy, and imagined her going out on dates with a better version of himself. He found comfort in repetition, which extended to playing the same piece of music many times over—"Burning Down the House," for example. Soon he stopped reading newspapers and kept an old one on his kitchen table, which greeted him with the same headline every morning ("Live Aid Broadcast Raises Millions For Africa"). He never took a day off from work, already unsure what to do with himself on the empty weekends.

As summer turned to fall Alex retained some hope that Susan and he would get back together, and sometimes it was enough to get him through another day. He hadn't acquired a taste for vodka but he drank it anyway. His bed was a futon for one. Usually he slept on the couch.

In October Alex's manager told him he was unimpressed with his job performance. "You're on autopilot, and I've no idea where you're heading," he said. "I doubt you know either."

"Being on autopilot must mean I'm flying," Alex said. "At least I've got that."

"What are you talking about?"

Alex thought for a moment. "I'll do better," he said.

Yet for the next month Alex did nothing more than show up at work, file reports in between daydreams, and then go home and drink. To avoid thinking of Susan, he created an imaginary woman and called her Suzanne. Physically she was based on a composite of two coworkers. As for her personality, she was loving, understanding, and forgiving. They shared the same interests, had similar hopes and fears.

Suzanne sighed happily. "You understand me."

"Of course I do. We're like two peas in a pod." She didn't ask if there were other peas in there with them.

Alex thought about her each night while trying to fall asleep. He imagined her falling in love with him. Eventually she asked him to marry her. All would have been well in his imaginary world, except by this time Suzanne had become Susan—physically, emotionally and in every other way. Then he gave up trying to imagine a better life with someone else.

He spent Thanksgiving getting drunk in his apartment, calling his parents to slowly express his regret at being unable to come home for the holiday.

Two weeks into January Alex's company fired him, or as his boss put it, "We're giving you the opportunity to pursue other opportunities." He had a series of temp jobs after that. By the fall he decided it was time to leave Baltimore, and began applying for positions in the D.C. area, eventually getting hired there as a financial analyst. He was starting over, and vowed to make serious changes in his behavior. He wanted to forget Susan, and decided the best way to do that was to become someone else.

Thus followed three straight years of varying New Year's resolutions.

1987 — THE YEAR OF READING BOOKS

Alex spent considerable time during the last week of 1986 developing his reading list for the new year. As a boy he read some fantasy and science fiction books, then lost interest in those subjects and gave up reading books altogether. Now he felt himself many years behind on his reading, and decided that if he dedicated himself to the task he could gain an understanding of the world, and that would take away his pain. Why should romantic love ever torture him again after he read the classics? He decided to read 52 books, one a week. With the aid of a great books list at the back of his college copy of Orwell's *1984*, he put 39 books on his list, including *The Great Gatsby*, *David Copperfield*, *The Philosophy of Nietzche*, *The Sound and the Fury*, a biography of Lincoln, Plato's *Republic*, *King Lear*, *The Letters of Thomas Jefferson*, *Herzog*, *Ulysses*, and *Lolita*. He left thirteen selections open for books that others might suggest to him during the year.

On New Year's Day 1987, hungry and hung over, he opened to page one of *The House of Seven Gables*. One week later he completed reading that book's introduction and put it aside to begin *Lolita*, which he read for two evenings until abruptly brought to a halt by a pressing matter (TV, NFL Playoffs). He then began and abandoned in turn two books on philosophy, three novels, and Lincoln's life. In late February his reading of *Tristam Shandy* was continually interrupted by the ticking of his front room clock. He read nothing outside of newspapers after that, and in June sold all his books, using the money to partially fund a VCR and a football.

1988 — THE YEAR OF DEPRAVITY

The Year of Depravity began at a New Year's Eve party. Alex left with the friend of a coworker and ended up at her apartment, finally going home at four in the afternoon two days later. He was surprised at his immediate success, though he did find the experience far less satisfying than expected. He also found it exhausting. On Friday nights he went out to bars, sometimes having to go to four or five before finding a woman willing to go home with him, if he found one at all, and he always seemed to need a drink.

One Friday evening in February he was drunk before 7:00 pm and left the bar with a woman in a leather jacket who said her name was Tracy or Lacy or Trixie. She came home with him and removed all her clothing, rolling it up in a ball and throwing it through his open window. They did things that Alex decided on the whole he would rather not do again. Late the next morning he woke up to find Tracy or Lacy or Trixie asleep beside him. He put on sweatpants and a t-shirt and went to the kitchen to eat a bowl of cereal. When he returned to his bedroom he found her standing beside the bed, steadying herself with a hand on the wall.

"I'm going to live here now," she said.

"I don't think that's such a good idea," he said. "To be perfectly honest, I don't even know your name."

"It's Lixie."

"Lixie? Your name is Lixie?"

"Not really. It's Lacy, but last night you kept calling me Lixie, so that will be your pet name for me."

Alex slumped to the floor and sat with his back against the wall. "Is it all right if I call you Susan?"

Lacy was inside his closet, looking through his clothes. She came out wearing his red flannel shirt and brown corduroy pants. "I don't think any of your shoes fit me."

Alex looked at her feet, certain that she was wearing his socks and wondering when she had put those on, and also wondering if she was wearing anything else of his that was currently hidden from view. "What do you say we go out for a bite to eat?"

"OK."

Alex drove Lacy to a restaurant that was near where she lived, or said she lived. They ate lunch with little conversation, Lacy occasionally smiling. She was pleasant throughout the meal, which only made Alex feel worse. He paid for the lunch, then told Lacy he was going to the bathroom. Once out the front door of the restaurant he ran to his car and drove away.

1989 — THE YEAR OF CLEAN LIVING

Alex decided The Year of Clean Living had to follow the Year of Depravity. He would cook his own meals at least five days a week and maintain a balanced and healthy diet. Every other day would be exercise day, which would eventually consist of running three miles plus doing fifty push-ups, once he got up the endurance. Every day he would mediate twice for fifteen minutes, once in the morning and again in the evening.

On New Year's Day 1989 Alex bought three shopping bags worth of new food and ingredients, intent on cooking a healthy meal sometime soon. On January 2 he went for a jog and sprained both his wrist and ankle when he lost his balance on a frozen puddle. On January 9 he fell asleep during his morning meditation and was several hours late for work. On January 11 he undercooked his vegetables and gave himself a mild though determined case of botulism. For the rest of the year he subsisted on pizza and beer while watching TV, sometimes contemplating what it all meant though never for long.

1990 — THE YEAR OF GETTING ENGAGED

Alex stared at the woman who sat down next to him on the train.

She glanced over. "Hello?"

"What? Oh, hello. Sorry, I thought I recognized you."

A brunette cut short, eyes wide as if she was pleasantly surprised by whatever she saw . . . For a brief wonderful and agonizing moment, he thought she was Susan.

He looked away.

The woman pulled a book out of her red carrying bag. Alex glanced at the title — *The Great Gatsby*. "That's a great book," he said, wishing he had said something clever, or at least used some word to describe it other than `great.' "I used to own it. Sold it to a used bookstore."

"I bought this one used."

"Maybe it's my old book?"

"Only if you wrote `Harmon was here' on the title page."

He shook his head. "I'm Alex. And I would never write `Alex was here' in a book."

"I'm Katie. Nice to meet you."

They talked about *The Great Gatsby*. Katie expressed her opinions and Alex agreed with her, not mentioning that he'd only read seven pages of it, and not all of those were consecutive. Later Katie turned to him and said, "This is my stop." He noticed her teeth then, messy in her mouth, a set that braces had never touched — just like Susan. He quickly asked for her phone number. She gave it. On their first date they went to lunch and later visited a used bookstore.

From then on they spoke several times a week and sometimes got together on the weekends, claiming they were just friends and continuing to make the claim to themselves and others well after it was no longer true. This meant they could see other people, which for Katie meant going out with several other men (Alex only dated Katie). She was invigorating, 5'2" of energy. And she set the agenda. As Alex thought of it, he was the one who started up the car, and then Katie drove - not literally, though sometimes that too.

One summer evening at a restaurant bar, Alex and Katie shared a glass of wine. "I'm beginning to like this decade," she said.

For Alex this would have been just another line in a

conversation, except that Katie said it while looking at him with affection. As if she was smitten. And that was the moment when Alex realized he was over his longing for Susan. It had been abating since meeting Katie, and now he confirmed it gone. All he needed, it seemed, was for someone to give him this look. All he needed was someone else.

"Here's to the nineties," he said, and he smiled and smiled.

Within days Alex had purchased an engagement ring, and the following weekend with ring in pocket he proposed to Katie. "Yes!" she said, and said it several more times. She called her parents, and then called someone named Brandon to cancel their date for the following night.

In the spring of 1991 Alex Rook and Katie Nelson got married at a rural church in Northeastern Ohio. Katie provided the bridesmaids and the groomsmen too, assigning her cousin as the best man.

A light rain began to fall during the outdoor reception, and then it poured. Alex considered this a good sign, even though all the guests had to move indoors and the forgotten wedding cake was getting soaked. Once inside Alex look around for his new wife, and then found himself staring at the closed bar. How could someone forget to keep the bar open during a wedding reception? Or had they decided to shut it down early to prevent someone having a few too many? Possibly he'd agreed to this, or possibly Katie had made this decision without his input. Except he wanted a drink right then and couldn't get one, just like that time some six years ago that he got off the road to read Susan's letter and found out the liquor store was closed. For the first time it occurred to him that he might well be within a few miles of that very store. He thought how odd life was, but not so bad in the long run.

With his hands in his pockets he went outside and stood under the front awning, looking out at the rain and imagining that the very same liquor store was within walking distance, that he could see the tops of the trees that lined the road next to the store, the trees he'd believed he would remember in detail all his life. But he was unsure. Did it matter? Not really, but it was interesting to think about. He stood outside by himself for fifteen minutes or more, watching the rain collapse his wedding cake into a lumpy puddle. It was difficult even for Alex to interpret that as a good sign, but struggling mightily, he managed it.

ELLA ON THE EDGE OF WINTER

> *. . . the image of hope is someone passing with a musical*
> *instrument in a case.*
> — *The Discovery of Heaven*, Harry Mulisch

A tall woman strides down the sidewalk
gripping a musical instrument case,
not large — an oboe? a clarinet?
        Almost no rain left hanging
in the air, though it rained all night.
Almost no shadows.

I should give her a season: mid-autumn.
With each gust, an arc of bright leaves
cascades down to scatter in her path
like applause.
        Others lie lumped at her feet —
muted shades of mahogany, gold,
blood-syrup — last night's leaves,
folded in on themselves.

It's morning, not late. No real hurry.
In this, there is always no hurry:
I've time to provide her an aging city center —
shop signs, pedestrians, cars at the curb

with overnight windows.

      Or is hers a small town —
a brick Presbyterian church, a sign reading
          Caution
        Children at Play,
a row of enfeebled saplings on First Street —
hedge maple? honey locust?

I try out some names she might have been given —
Elena, Jo, Kathleen. Maybe Ella?
She's not as young as I thought at first.
Shall I allow her the hint of a past — maybe
a previous season's losses?
Ella. Yes.
      She has turned
and is crossing a parking lot, climbing
three steps to a door at the rear
of the shop where she works.
Or an office?

Awkwardly, she shrugs from her coat
at the threshold —
her case changing hands — it's hard
to manage, and she sets it down
while she gathers herself.
Her raincoat drags on the floor.
      Inside, she is lost
for a moment to sight.
But only a moment.
She lockers her oboe as always

on Thursdays—her lesson
is just after closing.

Recently, she has considered quitting—
no passion, no great gift. Besides,
she's neglected her practice all summer.
Unhappiness has done this.
      Her workday begins.
She steps behind a counter
or among the shelves.
Straightening papers? Brewing, perhaps,
a cup of coffee?

It's here I'll leave her.

How, though, will she live out this day?
Who will remind her at quitting time
to cancel her lesson?
What will become of her instrument,
back in her tiny apartment?
      What will allow her to live
through the winter? And what
will become of me now,
having lost this piece, too, of my life?

BEGGARS

Lately I've been thinking about panhandlers, a fact of life in New York. Last week a girl in her twenties was slowly making her way through the subway car, listing the disasters that had befallen her which, she said, had left her homeless. The stories we hear are usually about a serious illness, death in the family, loss of job and shelter, a hungry child to feed. The girl began to pace from one end of the car to the other, imploring "Help me, HELP, HELP," until the words became a choking wail that filled the air. Most of us kept our eyes closed or fixed on our phones. I know that, because we, the entreated, are in this together, and that's why I steal furtive glances, wondering how others are, or aren't reacting. What should I think? Or do?

Describing my moral dilemma to a cousin, she recounted one of her own subway stories: an impeccably dressed man holding a clipboard described the tragedy of six-year-old girl in his neighborhood who had been killed — and her grieving parents didn't have enough money to bury her. "Could you find it in your hearts to help them out?" he asked. The tale elicited great sympathy and cash from the riders, many who appeared to be struggling themselves. "Oh no, a month later and she was killed again?" another passenger exclaimed in a tone of withering sarcasm, rolling his eyes. The exposure of this deception, followed by gasps and some laughter, caused the red-faced con man to rush out at the next stop.

That incident occurred years ago before the Transit Authority had produced its piped-in recording reminding passengers that soliciting money in the subway is illegal. "We ask you not to give," says the disembodied voice. "Please help us maintain an orderly subway." Another requests, "Please give instead to reputable charities."

And yet, my faith tells me that the needy are the face of God, and we must give food to the hungry, drink to the thirsty, clothes to the naked. That gets complicated in any big city when during the course of a day, a traveler may pass or personally encounter scores of beggars, some truly needy and others outright frauds. Even the deceivers are quick to say "God bless you" when accepting donations from sympathizers. It can be impossible to tell the difference between them.

I can still see the faces of some of the subway beggars I gave to, even years later — the man in tatters with one eye shut and the other bulging eye a startling milky-white and the man in a wheelchair with an ugly festering wound on his calf. With their physical deficits on display, I knew they weren't faking. Once I was overwhelmed by a beggar's dignified bearing that belied the humiliation of his silent supplication:

In the Land of Emperors[1]

He's alive, but halved, on a plank —
head, torso and muscled arms
wheeling down the train platform
to the top of the stairs,
and I stop in my tracks
midway through some rumination
that's instantly replaced by one
about humans made in God's own image.
I imagine the workbench abandoned
in the middle of the job,
some more cursed than others,
forced to eat dust,
denied the chance to run.
I reverse my steps,
read a billboard, wait till it's safe: he's gone.
Still, my legs quiver
on the same steep flight of steel steps
he bumped or slid or rode down
a moment ago, transporting himself
to the next plane, the broken world —
transforming himself.
In marble halls, I've admired
the busts of emperors, larger than life
with their smashed noses and missing limbs.
I know a black king
glides by now on ball bearings,
past sidewalk crowds that part in two.

---

[1] "In the Land of Emperors" was first published in *Dogwood* and appears in
A Secret Room in Fall (Ashland Poetry Press, 2006).

When was their last meal? Isn't it the duty of the privileged to feed those who hunger? I once passed a middle-aged woman beggar sitting on the sidewalk in an affluent Manhattan neighborhood. I was on my way to work, carrying my usual brown bag lunch. Passing her by, I remembered the turkey sandwich on multi-grain bread I'd made that morning, and retraced my steps. But when I handed her the foil-wrapped sandwich, she refused it, waving me away, a gesture that fed my cynicism, which seems always to lurk beneath the surface. Naturally, the sandwich was useless. It couldn't buy a bottle of gin or drugs.

Nothing left me feeling more uneasy than the two deaf Latino beggars who entered my subway car in Queens, an incident I remember clearly after two decades. They placed a cheap trinket on the lap of every seated passenger, along with a card announcing their disability and a request to buy their merchandise. As soon as that task was done, they returned to each rider, retrieving the cards and trinkets from those who didn't give. I remember how quickly they moved and how solemn they were, and the sadness mixed with disquiet that I felt watching them.

Later that year, a *New York Times* headline caught my eye: "Seven Arrested in Abuse of Deaf Immigrants." It turns out that those beggars—among a group of 57 including 12 children—had been victims of smugglers who brought them out of Mexico into New York with the false promise of an honest livelihood "working for a small business." Instead they were housed in a squalid apartment in Queens and forced to sell trinkets in the subway or face beatings, children included. At the end of the day, the money they brought in was turned over to the enforcers. Eventually, a few of the victims worked up the courage at 4 am to leave a letter about their plight at the local police station. I was upset to learn that this happened in my precinct and that these near-slaves had been hidden nearby.

If I'd felt uneasy witnessing those beggars in action—something beyond the fact of their begging seemed "off" to me—I was equally shaken by the victims' proximity to my home. Were there others hidden away from view, suffering terribly, in this place where I grew up, a community I thought I knew?

"The biggest factor that kept them there was their disability, which kept them dependent on the smugglers, and isolated them terribly," said an officer from Immigration and Naturalization Service. "That was their key vulnerability, and the smugglers exploited it tremendously." If I had bought a trinket that day, my money would have gone to the smugglers. But when the deaf beggars brought back too little, they were violently abused. Giving or not giving led to a negative outcome either way.

Like most New Yorkers, I've learned to trust my instincts and make a split-second decision as to whom I should give, knowing that I've probably made plenty of misjudgments over the years.

There are times when I give only because I feel pressured, which leaves me angry with myself and the person creating what I interpret as an implicit threat. Recently, sitting alone toward the end of an empty subway platform, I was approached by a teenage boy with a mask-like, forlorn expression. He came so close that when he extended his open palm, his skin almost touched my face. Aware at that moment of my isolation, I reached into my handbag, careful not to bring my wallet into view, handing him a dollar. Without a word, he swaggered away. His sudden change of gait confirmed my suspicion: I'd been had. Before I could dwell on what had just occurred, a wiry, street-wise-looking guy with earbuds and a backpack appeared on the adjoining bench.

"Did he bother you?" he asked me. "I don't like that shit. I was watching from down the platform and was ready to move in if I had to." I thanked him for his concern, silently grateful for the presence of invisible guardians in our midst.

For the first time in a lifetime of exposure to city beggars, I've just encountered a subway poet, "Brian from the Bronx." Dressed neatly in black jeans and a pressed white t-shirt, Brian recited from memory a long, rhyming, lyrical poem about his life and his yearning to become someone who mattered. I only wish I could have recorded the work of this talented writer who was so modest, he didn't even extend his hand as he walked through the car. We could have been at the events corner of Barnes & Noble.

And then there are the musicians. "I don't beg. I entertain New York," the stout old man announced yesterday, smiling broadly and then launching into a one-man version of the Drifters' "Under the Boardwalk," followed by other sixties soul hits. I have a soft spot for all musicians — the Irish folk singer and her companion fiddler, the Andes natives in multi-colored serapes playing pan flutes, the gray-haired doo-woppers moving their hands and feet in choreographed harmony, the electric guitarists backed by a wildly expressive violinist, the blues singer as moving as B.B. King, the man tapping a Chinese xylophone gently, as if freeing its spirit, the teenager wearing a gown ideal for a Met debut singing an aria from *La Traviata* — all the world's music amplified and resonating in the subway's passageways.

Of course, buskers don't consider themselves beggars. I wonder if my Italian-born ancestors living in Manhattan in the early 1900s ever gave a coin to an organ grinder with or without a trained monkey wearing perfectly stitched, handmade clothes? Many of those performers were poor immigrants from Southern Italy who eked out a living for their families, playing and replaying the same few stored tunes. But that ended in 1935 when Mayor LaGuardia banned them, considering the organ grinders to be beggars who added clutter to New York's teeming streets.

In the era of boom boxes, the subways were filled with b-boys blasting their favorite funk tunes while they breakdanced with abandon down the aisle. Although I was impressed with the energy and gymnastic skill on display, I have to admit at the risk of sounding like a grouch that I resented their attitude of domination. "It's show time! We're here and we're great!" It may not ever be completely peaceful underground, hurtling with all kinds of strangers in a no-exit situation, but we are usually left alone with our private thoughts, our music, our reading, our endless digital distractions. Not true with the breakdancers whose act takes over our space. We're suddenly with them on the narrow stage of the subway car, like it or not. I think some passengers quickly pay up just to be rid of them.

My attitude hadn't changed when the newest version of

subway performer recently appeared in my car: a teenager with one of those trendy blonde Afros who first turned on the music (to my surprise, a long-ago disco hit—loud, but not ear-splitting) and then catapulted his lithe body onto the looped metal rods attached to the ceiling. His acrobatic maneuvers were astonishing. He, too, took over the car, and his quick moves overhead in the tight space made me duck a few times. And yet, in spite of myself, I couldn't help admiring his exuberance and ability to defy gravity like a ballet dancer or Olympic gymnast. And then, head dangling upside down, he reached out and lightly touched the finger of a seated woman. She allowed a faint smile to cross her face.

In the land of beggars, even those who have no legs still manage to overcome the limitations of their bodies. And at least one, I've witnessed, can fly.

MAN OF SCIENCE

I pinch the pinchy-part of my prescription pill bottle and shuck one onto the coffee table. Then I flatten it with my credit card and vacuum up two quick lines, one for each nostril. Tilting back my head, I saw at the underside of my nose. There, I think, much better.

With Harold out breaking parole, drinking a thousand beers, a thought around here actually stands a chance. "Bottoms up," I say. Once I would've wasted my breath. But without a prison sentence looming, I'm afraid, he's lost all brotherly incentive — drinking and carousing again, plucking at my nerves like he swore he wouldn't. His latest is: "Go out and get some sun, Wade. I can see your organs shining through." The silence is golden.

Under the right conditions, I really am quite capable. I can connect ideas with such complexity if you shined a light into one ear, in through the prism of my brain, a brilliant rainbow would project out the other side.

Even if my ex-lab assistant, Lizzie, says I'm a dope fiend.

"You're a dope fiend," I hear her say. And I look over at her empty indentation at the other end of the couch as if she'd really said it, half-expecting to find her rat's nest hair floating there above a textbook, shiny black eyes cutting me with judgment. Then, I recall, she's home tonight, packing for Africa, that in a couple more days, her worry will be continents away.

"Good riddance," I tell her empty indentation on the couch as I shuck out another pill. Then I flatten it, vacuum up two more lines. And while I know it's highly unusual for an organism to actively seek out punishment, paradoxically, as I saw at the underside of my nose, I long for her to chide me, for Lizzie to call me a dope fiend.

Then the postnasal drip drips down the back of my throat, and I am ready. I pull the coffee table closer, adjust my glasses, poise my fingers over the keyboard as the cursor's pixels sizzle in and out and my genius begins to whir . . .

And I can feel it right there on my fingertips, about to explode across the keyboard at any minute, any second, with the final strokes of my Magnum Opus, *Anthropometric Correlates of Foot-size in Females*, when my cell phone suddenly break-dances off the coffee table into my lap, startling me all to hell.

Lizzie —

Don't you dare pick that up, I tell myself. It's Friday night and Harold is out. You're granted this rare silence, with your thesis defense only weeks away and all these important knots still left to unwind, that once unwound will open new worlds for you. Do not pick up that phone, Wade.

I say, "Hello?"

And Lizzie says, "Hi."

Then the connection fizzles briefly between us. Yet after the fizzling clears, a mysterious piece remains, low and rhythmic and rumbling. A male's voice, perhaps? And I wonder if Lizzie has a boyfriend she hasn't told me about, if perhaps she'd withheld the news because she thought it'd hurt me, because she thought I was that lonely. Then, suddenly, I'm wondering all sorts of things — about his name and IQ points, about if they plan to stay together while she studies big cats in Africa. I wonder: Is that a British accent I hear? And as I wonder, an inexplicable current of dread competes with this wondering, overtakes it like a race horse—because, suddenly, it's like I'm the only person in the entire world who's never known love and affection.

Then a wildcat roars, and I realize my mistake—that Lizzie's "boyfriend" is only David Attenborough narrating about a pack of starving lionesses, episode three from Planet Earth. I breathe out in a whoosh. And Lizzie says, "Wade, I can hear you breathing!" letting loose a laugh that flits about my ears like a bird.

When the sound dies away, I don't want it to stop.

So, I make my breath wet, choppy, like a pervert calling in the night. Hunching over the coffee table, I breathe in and out, in and out. And a few pervy breaths is all it takes: Lizzie basically falls to pieces again, laughing and laughing until I need to step in for her health.

"Lizzie," I say, "that's quite enough. Harold is out and I should really utilize this peace and quiet."

After a while, she manages to pull herself together. "I just wanted to remind you that I'm leaving the day after tomorrow," she says.

And I say, "Knowing is preferable to not knowing."

To which she exclaims, "My favorite assumption of science! But seriously, Wade, I was afraid I wouldn't catch you. I said to myself, 'Lizzie tonight is the night Wade decides to hit the town.' I said, 'Tonight is the night he puts the thesis aside.'"

Then it's my turn to laugh. We both do, both knowing I never leave the apartment.

And as our laugher dovetails together, I can feel my self-control melting away. The tiny clock in the right-hand corner of my monitor flinches, and I know my precious quiet is slipping away, that any minute Harold will return and slow all progress to a crawl.

However, despite my better judgment, despite having much more important knots to unwind, I lean back into the comfy crook of the couch, and say, "Lizzie, are you familiar with the recent discoveries surrounding the Golden Ratio in nature?"

And just like that, we're chatting with unstoppable momentum.

Over the next hour, we light upon every topic: everything from Semen Displacement theory to alternative theories of Dinosaur Extinction, contagious yawning to mate-guarding in the modern age. We prattle on with passion.

As I explain the test for animal self-awareness, I imagine a blood-streaked lioness prowling across her glistening eyes: "Gordon Gallup Jr. invented it in the seventies," I say. "He trained a monkey to look at itself in a mirror. Then he anesthetized the aforementioned monkey and proceeded to put an odorless dot on its forehead. He would then awake the monkey and if the monkey regarded the dot in the mirror, behold, a self-aware monkey." I am nearly breathless when I finish, and evidently so is Lizzie.

Nearly breathless, she says, "And has this test been done with other animals?"

"Dolphins are self-aware," I say. "Magpies, elephants, chimpanzees as well, among few others."

"Are dogs self-aware?" she asks.

"Dogs are not."

"Surely cats, then?"

"Not them, either."

"Is Harold self-aware?"

"Is an earthworm self-aware?" I say. Then we both go in stitches all over again, with Lizzie spraying laugher like fresh sunshine.

It doesn't take long for her to recover her seriousness, however. An idea has struck her: "It seems this test has an inherent bias toward the sighted," she says. "What about bats or blind catfish found deep in cave systems? What about deep sea fish with pale and chalky eyes?"

This seems like a point to consider, and I tell her so. "That has thesis written all over it," I say as my mind rolls over the word *thesis* like a bump, causing my eyes to scan the bookish clutter laid before me: the desperate scrawl of my note-taking, my toppled prescription pill bottles and rolled up dollar bill, the dead-glowing eye of my laptop—and, suddenly, it's all like some sort of prison I must escape.

I say I have to go.

"Wait," Lizzie replies. "One more thing. Dinner tomorrow? At my place. To say goodbye?"

But with all of my work it's an impossibility—she knows that. "I simply can't make it," I say. "But seriously, Lizzie, have a nice time in Africa . . ." Then there's a long, heavy silence, after which I think to add, "But please beware of brain eating amoebas and fleshing-eating worms," which, of course, is another joke.

But for whatever reason, only a cold and barren silence emanates from her end as I hang up the cell phone—no laughter at all.

Later that night or, more accurately, earlier that morning, Harold comes home wrecked out of his mind. I can tell by the way he struggles with the lock. Part of me hopes he'll give up and go sleep on the curb like a garbage can. But he's determined, and eventually his footsteps spill into the apartment like a hailstorm of bowling balls.

"Wade!" he calls out. "Oh, Wade!"

Listening, I pray for the comforting creak of his bedroom door, the crunch of cot-springs, but instead I hear something troubling: footsteps on the attic stairs. Just in time, I manage to stash my Adderall paraphernalia under a heap of papers before his head floats up along with the rest of his apish form, a six-pack dangling from his wrist.

Then he just teeters there a while, wobbly and loose. When he finally tries to speak, the alcohol stitches his words together into one long, brutish grunt at which I have to tilt my ear like a dog to understand.

"No, Lizzie is at home, packing for her trip," I tell him.

Then he grunts some more, imploring vaguely sexual ideas with his hands.

"Why would I be over there?" I say. "We're only friends."

Then Harold grunts, gestures some more.

And I say, "Yes, Harold. I'm glad you're glad I'm still awake." But I don't know why he's surprised. Ever since he moved back in, I've been doing nothing but ruining my posture at this coffee table.

However, I don't have time to explain this all again. I've got bigger knots to unwind—and I'm about to tell him so, to give him the usual lecture about the growing strains of our cohabitation, about the perils of his thoughtlessness and self-abuse, about the values of hard work, dedication, when a girl in a silver and shivering sequin dress steps up beside him.

Clarissa —

I blink, blink again, yet there she stands, teetering right along with him.

"This is my friend Clarissa," Harold then informs me, as if I didn't know. "And this is my twin brother, Wade. Isn't he handsome?"

And Clarissa says, "My, you two are mirror images."

"Minus the tattoos and prison biceps, of course," he says, laughing.

Then Clarissa extends her hand in greeting. And by the way her fingers unfurl, I can tell she doesn't remember — that in her drunken state she doesn't recall the entire semester we spent together in evolutionary psychology four years prior, doesn't recall all the times I tutored her free of charge, did her homework, and signed her name for attendance when she was too hung-over to attend, the way in which I tilted my exams for her to steal a glance or how, on the last day of class, I worked up the courage to ask her out, and she called me, "Creepy, pathetic, weird."

It was a crushing blow. Harold was living with me at the time, and I remember telling him about the incident in a fit of upset. "I thought the evolutionary paradigm was shifting from brawn to brains," I told him. "I thought she really liked me!" "You know what your problem is?" he replied. Anticipating one of his usual punch lines, I said: "That no one is interested in a twenty-something with a bald spot, hairless boy chest, and hands as soft as veal cows?" But for once he didn't appear to be joking. Reaching out, he touched my shoulder like he was about to drop some brotherly knowledge: "You over-think everything and lack the most basic instincts." I'm sure he took my silence for appreciation, but that's the thing my brother always forgets: I'm basically allergic to human contact, that I get itchy and squirm at the slightest touch. In our youth, he used to hug me until I passed out cold.

"Don't be rude," Harold urges me in the attic. "Shake Clarissa's hand!"

But try as I do, I cannot. My throat is so dry and useless that I can't even remind him of my aversion to human touch.

After so much of this, he attempts to nudge the conversation along. "Wade is a Ph.D. candidate at the university," he explains.

And Clarissa says, "That's right. Harold was telling me all about you." She then withdraws her hand and snaps her fingers, as if trying to remember something.

Then I watch Harold's hand slip around her waist with such ease and whisper something in her ear that causes her eyes to light up with her remembering.

"Harold tells me you're doing a study on feet?" she says.

And I cannot believe it. "*Anthropometric Correlates of Facial Attractiveness in Females,* actually," I say, my voice coming loose for the talk of science.

"I promised her you'd give her a summary," Harold says.

And I say, "How nice of you," feeling truly touched, because it's about time Harold takes an interest, it's about time someone other than Lizzie appreciated all my hard work.

Then I can't help it—I just erupt: "My hypothesis is quite controversial," I say. "It plays off the myth of the female hunter. Familiar? It's a little-known fact that women are better long-distance runners than men, and my hypothesis piggybacks off the theory that women, even pregnant women, hunted quite readily in prehistoric times. See, it all has to do with foot-size and its relationship to the lower spine, the sacrum. Paradoxically, the smaller the better in terms of fitness. I wish I had my calipers on hand, Clarissa. I'd love to measure your feet. Do you happen to know your BMI offhand? Your foot-size? Can you attest to a highly carnivorous appetite? . . ."

I go on for quite a while, at tops speed—unable to help myself and glad to share the intrigue of the findings of all my hard work.

However, as I finish up, their faces are not as I imagined: not masks of amazement at all. In fact, they seem set to explode, with the edges of their mouths fluttering, like valves attempting to relieve the mental pressure of their not-understanding. Then I realize: I've done that thing I do when I get excited, I've shot right off to the moon at speeds that only the likes of Lizzie can follow.

So, I begin another rendition of my theory, this time at a slower pace and with sharper diction and smaller words for comprehension. "My hypothesis is quite controversial," I say at quarter-speed. "It plays off the myth of the female hunter . . ."

However, not long into this second attempt, Harold cuts me off with sudden laugh. They both do. And as their laughters crash into me like a rogue wave, I realize that once again I've walked right into another one of Harold's jokes, that I've misread all the cues.

"He really does sound like a robot," Clarissa says.

"I told you," Harold replies, still laughing.

And I shudder once, and am frozen. Suddenly, I'm fifteen

again, back in biology class, in chemistry, in calculus, and I've done that thing I do when I cannot stop myself and the entire class reacts as if I'm some kind of freak. And I want to tell them all—I want to scream!—"Don't you know the evolutionary paradigm is shifting!? Don't you know that things will one day be different?"

Then Harold is touching me—touching me and saying, "Wade, snap out of it. It was just a joke." But his hands like great leeches sucking at my neck. His breath a hot snake in my ear as he tries to shake me quiet.

"Let me go!" I say. Yet, even as I squirm, he holds tight.

"Calm down. We were just having a laugh," he says. "We actually came up here to ask you to join us. Come on down, will you? Do you want to call Lizzie? We've got beer, it's Friday night. What could be wrong? Put the thesis aside for a while, brother. Forget about this stuff for a little while . . ."

But at this point—even if I didn't have all this work!—I couldn't if I wanted to. Under Harold's touch, every last one of my molecules has hardened. I'm in full lock-down mode and can do nothing but stand there frozen as they descend the stairs.

"Well, if you change your mind," Harold calls back. Then they are gone.

And for a while, I can do nothing but listen to the slamming of cabinet doors, the microwave powering on and off, and the murmur of their conversation. The tinkle of their laughter, the sound of them finishing the last of my frozen pizza supply while I just stand there frozen with this knot tightening in my brain. And the knot is this: What does Harold have that I don't?

However, after a while the pizza smell that wafts up works me over. Like a solvent, it begins to de-thaw my hunger. My stomach rumbles. I haven't eaten all day, I realize.

Maybe I did over-react, I think. Maybe Harold really was just playing a joke, I tell myself, rising to my feet and taking a step. Maybe walking away will allow me to finally unwind these final, pesky knots.

Then I stop dead—because just like that the conversation and chewing downstairs has cut off, and a strange silence is suddenly rising the stairs. When I cock my ear to listen, I hear it: the wet, sloppy sound of their kissing lips, the pleasurable grunts of their groans. I hear Harold getting the affection I worked so hard for with the slightest of ease, as if no thought were necessary or involved.

Early the next morning, I start cleaning, still unable to figure it out: What Harold has that I don't. Tattoos and prison biceps, sure. The speech patterns of a Neanderthal? Yet, with all my smarts, I cannot figure it out. Not with all these pizza crusts and beer cans and cast aside clothes strewn about the place, anyway.

So, I parachute a fifty-gallon garbage bag and start collecting garbage. Then I sponge off the crumby counters. I Swiffer the floors, getting up the dust. And I must admit that, as I do this, I feel my stress levels subside.

When I'm all finished, I know, the kitchen will sparkle and resemble a time long before Harold when my ecosystem was distraction free. When a guy could think. After a few quick lines, I tell myself, everything will be just fine. You'll be able to push this all from your mind.

But then Harold's door swings open into the kitchen and he emerges in the nude, scratching himself. "Morning little brother," he grumbles, voice choppy with sleep, and my hope goes to shit. He picks up a crust of pizza I must've missed, chews on it lazily.

Then he just stands there, naked, waiting for me to chide him.

And I do—I can't help but say, "I wish you'd cover up, damn it."

To which he replies: "But we're mirror images, brother. You've seen all this before!" before proceeding to knock at his brain while shaking his wang in my general direction. Then, once he's finished, he stumbles off into the bathroom, where he proceeds to take a piss I think will never end. On and on, it goes, in an endless waterfall—a territorial piss meant to drive me out. To get me gone. And, suddenly, I just can't take it, anymore. I throw the Swiffer down and flee into the blinding, x-ray light of day.

Despite the early hour, the city is already stirring. People are out on their stoops, playing dominos, drinking beer. "Nice day," they tell me. "Spring has sprung," they say.

But do I return their salutations? No, I just drift along—pale as a ghost—articulating my woes in a sublingual fashion. "What does Harold have that I don't?" I say. "What does Harold have that I don't?"

Articulating, I wander down Madison, past the restaurants, where people are already out sipping mimosas from patio chairs. I wander up New Scotland, past the hospital, where they are already out in hospital gowns and wheelchairs, soaking in the sun like potted plants. At last finding myself in Washington Park, on a park bench, bumping bumps of the last of my Adderall off the hinge in my hand, and I still cannot figure it out.

Dog-walkers pass by on the trail, bike riders and couples holding hands so effortlessly with love. A ragged bum passes, pushing along a shopping cart, and even he seems happy with his affairs in the world. It's like they've all got it so figured out.

At dusk, I call Lizzie, sunburnt from exposure, buzzing with drugs.

I'd have preferred the warm computer glow of my thesis, but Lizzie's is the next best thing. If I looked Harold in the eye, I'm now certain, I'll be rendered forever powerless, the beta twin.

"Lizzie," I say. "You're my final hope. Is your offer still on the table?"

And she replies: "Yes, of course, you can still come over. I'm so glad you called."

And I do. I come over — moments later, in fact, I'm there, knocking at the door of her brownstone.

Fresh out of the shower, she then answers the door, wet and flushed. I barely recognize her. Her rat's nest hair, no longer a rat's nest: flattened down in this attractive mane that lies across her scalp. Instead of her usual university t-shirt, she's donned a sleeveless floral dress. Even her smile is different.

"Lizzie?" I say.

"You look like hell, Wade," she replies, all differently.

When she leans in for a hug, I shy away. Mostly, I can tolerate brief human contact with people I trust, but this is all too much. "Come inside already," she says and laughs a laugh that even sounds different.

And I do. I follow her into the living room and collapse onto the couch where I stare vacantly all the animal posters on the wall. And the wildebeest and zebras and lionesses and Meerkats all stare right back. "Are you alright?" she asks me.

"I had a rough night!" I say.

To which Lizzie gives me a half-jealous, half-heart-broken stare.

"You liar," she says. "You said never went out! Where did you go? You should've called."

And I say, "I didn't go out drinking. I don't. You know, I never leave the house!" Then, stammering and probably speaking too fast for even for Lizzie, I swing into the whole explanation. And she sits down next to me to listen, nodding along. A bottle of wine manifests. She pours some as I tell her everything: about Harold and Clarissa, how I cannot understand the signs. I say, "What does Harold have that I don't?" I say, "How can a Ph.D. candidate be so stupid?" I say a lot of things to provide all the facts to form a hypothesis, so she can help me understand.

However, when I finish, all Lizzie does is swirl her wine glass and look beseechingly into its purple vortex. She crosses, re-crosses her legs. And despite my nerves, I cannot help but steal a glimpse of her toes. I watch them bunch and flex like exotic fruit, and am stricken nearly breathless by their unexpected beauty. I've never noticed.

Then she turns to me with a true bruised hurt in her eyes, and says, "Does this means you didn't really want to see me. That you're just avoiding Harold?" And I just freeze.

You idiot, I think. You've gone and hurt the girl. You're supposed to be an expert on human behavior, and this is how you behave? Like some animal scrambling for safety, you thought no further than a place to hide.

The seconds drag by awkwardly. My mouth goes cinnamon dry. I know I should say really something — that I'm sorry, that I'd wanted to come all along, anything — but my throat won't allow a word.

For a moment, I think Lizzie might ask me to leave. But then the timer in the kitchen dings and she excuses herself to check on dinner as if nothing has occurred. And as her high heels click away on the hardwood floors, I am grateful. I wonder why she has always been so nice to me. I wonder why she wanted to see me so bad, why my omission about Harold and Clarissa appeared to her hurt. But the more I wonder, the tighter the knots inside my brain become.

Returning with a serving tray, Lizzie equips the coffee table with the spread of spaghetti and meatballs and candlesticks with long white stems before positioning herself across from me. Then we begin to eat without speaking a word. We're both veritable encyclopedias of knowledge, yet neither of us seems able to think of anything to discuss.

My throat becomes so dry I tuck the food into my cheeks like a squirrel. When I try to smile, a string of marinara dribbles down my chin. I look at my plate, unable to swallow. I look at the walls, the animals plastered there: the rhinos, the Rhesus monkeys, the Spring Bocks leaping into the air. And they all stare at me in accusation.

"I feel like we're sitting in a watering hole," I try to joke. But my voice is too forced, too tremulous, and I can hear the fraudulence as Lizzie laughs.

I fork another meatball into my mouth. Another.

I don't want her to go. For the next few months, I don't want this incident stuck in her craw. But what can I do? Any moment, I expect her to make up some excuse and tell me to leave, to never contact her again. I can feel her gaze bearing into me.

But where, and at what? My mind is filled with questions. My nose? My mouth? My squinty little eyes?

"Do I have something stuck in my teeth?" I say, mouth full of food.

"No, I don't think so," Lizzie replies.

But, suddenly, I don't believe her. I gulp the food down and nearly choke to death then I begin slashing at the gaps in my teeth with a fingernail. I'm glad to have something to do, something tangible, a concrete problem to solve. And I must admit, doing this, I feel a little better. "Did I get it?" I say.

"I still don't see anything," she replies.

But from her face I can tell she's lying, and I keep slashing. "Better?" I say.

"All better," she lies — I know it, her voice is thick with it. "Just take it easy, Wade," she says, removing a small compact mirror from her purse and handing it to me. "See?"

After careening the small circular reflection around my teeth, however, I don't see. I don't see anything — yet I know it's there, that Lizzie is messing with me, like they always do. When the pebble of laughter falls from her mouth, that's confirms it. I stare down at the carnage on my plate, tasting blood. And even though her laughter quickly dies away, I can still hear it, echoing around the prism of my brain. I don't speak for what could be seconds, minutes, or even hours. I can feel my molecules hardening, full shut-down mode coming on, to ruin everything.

So, before it's too late, I excuse myself and break for the bathroom in a galloping run. "Wade," she calls after me. "Stop!" But I am gone. I can't stop — at least not until I'm safe to position myself before the medicine cabinet's mirror and see for myself. Not until I know.

In the mirror, I smile hugely, part my lips, and commence searching the wedges of my teeth. However, much to my surprise, I find nothing. There's only my sunburnt and exhausted reflection, repeatedly groping away at bloody gums, committing the same kind of self-abuse I've been lecturing Harold about all these years.

I stop my slashing, drop my Adderall-quivering hands, and it's my twin brother I see. I see him drunk and jobless and teetering. But I also see him satisfied, free. I see him constantly laughing despite the facts. And I see the wisdom in that. And it's like his laughter bursts out of me. Suddenly, I feel possessed. As I laugh, I start to beat my chest in a Congo rhythm, like a far-off tribal drum to herald my descent into madness. I can hear another drum beat coming for me from down the hall, too, like a beast of prey. And I know I've finally lost it. That I am gone.

But then, strangely, I hear the drumbeat pass the bathroom door, and the front door slams.

"Lizzie?" I call out. I crack the door, call again.

But I know she's gone. And how can I blame her? She's about to leave for three months, and this is the goodbye I give her. I should've realized, I should've read the signs. All this studying, all of this time together, and still I know nothing of human behavior. I've been looking in all the wrong places, I realize. All along it's been written on my forehead in a big red dot: Desire! Desire! Desire!

And just like that, I've gone truly primal. If Harold has ever done a thing for me, it's push me to this breaking point. Suddenly, I'm drunk with instinct, alight with colors and sounds. I give over to my muscles as they carry me out the front door after her. And on the stoop, I stand there sniffing the breeze — a honing pigeon, a tracking wolf, a bloodhound. My nose flexes after her scent, catching hints of dandelions riding the air. My olfactory bulb whirs, calculating her direction with ease. Then I set off in an eastern run without a single thought. Nothing. I don't think about what I'll say to her. And it doesn't matter. I'm past all that now. When I catch her, I'll gather her in my arms and we will touch, and touch, and touch.

RAYNALD PATRICE DESMEULES NAYLER

I RAN AWAY BUT SOME, BY CHOICE, REMAIN—

I ran away but some, by choice, remain—
content even to rent in neighborhoods
where once their parents owned. When childhood
ends—the haunted air and gnomèd mine—
what's left is bowling alleys and the steakhouse
Friday (*Timor Mortis conturbat me*),
the moon-drunk dogs that howl at passing trains,
Mason jars of bolts and ordered tools
neatly lined up on the pegboard wall
of a cricket-loud garage. Here once
a father sanded down a soapbox car,
spun its wheels, and held it to a son.
A distant engine roars. Along the drive
the rose beds keep the long day's heat alive.

BIRD WATCHING ON THE MADISON

Forty wingbeats wide for a mallard,
a straight roll through sagebrush prairie
on perpetual migration north,
this river is made for birds:
Northern shovelers, pelicans, geese glide
upriver, down. They rest. They drift.

I still my oars, attention stolen
by the meadowlark singing from the sage
and in response a blackbird's churr
in the willows. They're repeated,
call and answer, insistent
as if each yearns to convince the other
its way is best.

The lark is wing flash and wild song, trilling
the shapes of the seven winds,
how his wings carve the sky,
and how someday he will master
the golden path to the sun.

Blackbird's dreams are the sound of wind
rattling the cattails
and she responds: Observe

the sweet marsh grass, how water
shines and wanders. Consider
the white grubs found in roots of willows.

I don't know which way your heart turns
but if you come with me on this river,
endless as prairie wind, I hope
it will win you over, too, Kathleen.

A PACKET OF ARTHRITIS PILLS

This is Jeanine Cohen. She reminds me of my grandmother. That pale, almost translucent roundish face, the lash-less eyes, those thin colorless lips. See the vague upturn there at the corner of her mouth, the way she looks like she's almost smiling? There's a sort of peace in that. Like she's rising above a bad dream, a forgetfulness. I think they'd all like to do that, don't you? I mean forget about life. Just get out. She's been here since two weeks ago last Friday. Final tortured stages of cervical cancer. She'll be gone soon.

My grandmother had an aneurysm in her abdomen. She went fast. But before they let her go, they'd sit her up in a chair in the nursing home — two days before she died. And they *made* her eat. God awful, don't you think? This woman rode horses when she was eighty, and went solo trekking to Bhutan. She couldn't even pee anymore or lift a fork. But they put her in that chair and they *made* her eat.

That was almost ten years ago now. I was only nine or ten, but I remember going into the room with my mother and seeing grandma propped up in one of those god-awful chairs with the little iron wheels? Her eyes were black slits. I don't think she knew who I was. But she looked up when I came in and there was this kind of plea on her face. I'll never forget it.

Mrs. Cohen here's nearly eighty-eight. She's had a good long life, I think. Ending it shouldn't be such a trial or an ordeal.

I'm giving it a lot of thought. Wouldn't you?

My mom and dad used to take us down to visit grandma when we were little, at least once a year, down to Delhi by Lake Erie. Toronto's just too sprawling for her. She said she got hives, but I don't think so. I mean Bhutan's no picnic. It's farm country down there, you know.

Delhi, I mean. She went there to cool her heels between adventures she used to say. I always stayed at her house when everyone else was across the road at my uncle's. She had a pump in her kitchen. Can you believe it? A pump. In the kitchen. And pillow cases she embroidered herself. I could feel bumps from the stitching on my fingers at night. We used to play cribbage and she'd fix me warm milk before I went to bed, heated on her wood stove. I slept a lot better down there than I ever did at home. My mom just didn't have the time for that. Never did. Still doesn't, I guess.

I've worked here nearly two years now and I always learn a lot from these old ladies. Take Mrs. Bellevue down the hall in 3llC. What good is it to anybody to have her lying there incontinent and blind? She's got Alzheimer's and I mean *real* bad. Didn't know who I was the other day. Told me she wanted to go home. Back to Pittsburgh. Teach piano again. Well, I knew what she meant. Don't we all? Wanting to go home, I mean. Some safer afterlife, eh? Who wants to feel like their brains are being sucked out, you know what I mean?

I was in there last night and watched her a long time in the dark. She looked like a corpse, all swathed up in white cotton sheets, stinking like old lady, bed sores and urine. She opened her eyes once and I saw this awful blankness there, like she was some half-dead animal caught in a trap. My grandmother had that same hopelessness on her face.

The woman that was in that room before her, Celia Martin, I think it was, she had that same horrid look just before she went. I mean, it was a real blessing when her oxygen failed.

Before I came here, I worked two years in the emergency room at Sick Kids. We had some real close calls there. It took a toll on everyone. It's not easy being the one who watches them all suffer. I mean doctors come and doctors go and even the RNs. A shot here, a shot there, lay out the meds, bark out the orders. But we CNAs, we do all of the grunt work. We're the ones up-close and personal, changing the bed pans and the diapers, cleaning butts and bed sores. Somebody's gotta do it.

My mom couldn't even be on the ward without going all squishy. Queasy-like. What a burden for families to have children in such a state, she always said. She had a hard enough time of it with us normal kids. I remember once when we were all under eight — there's four of us, me, my older sister, Mandy, and the twins, Cara and Crystal — she took us to the park once and left us there. At least that's how I remember it. I mean she was gone for hours.

Mandy told me years later that she'd gone to meet some boyfriend, some sailor, 'cause dad was on the road. He was some kind of salesman. Insurance, I think. Anyway, he was gone all the time. That's all I remember. I don't believe her though. Mandy, I mean. Moms don't do that sort of thing, do they? Leave their kids alone. Well, no, I'm not that big a baby. But *my* mom wouldn't do it, eh? Grandma wouldn't have done it.

Jane Harris here had a massive stroke in a nursing home about a week ago. Skinny as a bean, she is. Can't even eat on her own anymore. They feed her with a tube. She's a mess any which way you look at it. Her family can't seem to see their way to cutting off her food and water. But she shouldn't have to lie around here like that much longer. Not if I can help it.

Grandma was poorly in the end too, of course. We didn't go down to see her as much as we used to. I don't know why, really. Maybe it was just too much trouble for mom. Probably. I mean, Grandma was in and out of the hospital and then into that god-awful nursing home.

She told me once that I should look into nursing. All that blonde hair of yours, Brook, she'd say. You'd look good in white. Ha! Like that's any part of it, eh? But I *do* look good in white. I don't go much for all those colored scrubs with dogs and cats and balloons and seashells and teddy bears. That kind of shit. Unprofessional, I think. I mean, white has a purity to it, don't you think? You can keep your distance in white. It's clean. It's simple. It's straightforward. The color of truth, I think. There's black. And then there's white.

When I first finished my CNA training I thought, well, yeah, now I can do my bit to help make people's lives a bit easier, you know. But it doesn't happen that way much, at least it doesn't for me. But I think now, that as long as there's so much pain in healing, I'd see about making those hurting a bit more whole again in some way. You know what I mean? Not just slapping on a gauze bandage or swabbing dry lips. I can make the inevitable easier on everyone, less of a torment. Hospice work is really satisfying that way.

Take Mrs. Samolus next door. She's one of my favorites. She was brought here from a convalescent home outside of Drayton. Dementia. She's ninety-two. And bed sores? How nice can that be, eh? We have to turn her two, maybe three times a day, when we can get around to it. We've got a lot on our plates, you know. See here on her chart? They've prescribed arthritis pills? Arthritis pills! Can you imagine? You're gorked out in some steel-armed bed in a room full of nothing, unless you count the god-awful drone of that iron-lung oxygen machine over there. And they're worried about arthritis?

I took the last packet of pills with me on a picnic to Toronto Island with my boyfriend, Ralph. We've been going out since senior high. Ralph's ok for the time being. But he's junk really, on the nerdy side. You know what I mean? All these idiot puns flying out of his face morning and night. I aim to snag me a doctor in time, no doubt about it. Don't laugh.

Anyway, Ralph has a kinda cruel way about him at times. Like we were making our way to the back of the island and I don't know if you've been there or not, but they have these signs, 'Please Walk on the Grass,' eh? I think that's awesome, so I'm just about to head across. We're going to the other side anyway, where the paddle boats are. And old Ralph has this hissy fit. If everybody did that there'd be no grass at all. Yadda, yadda, yadda. That kind of shit. Well, that's just stupid. Why the hell put a sign like that up if you don't mean it? So anyway, we walked way the hell around. But I was telling him about old Mrs. Samolus and he got all frothy and worked up about those arthritis pills. Said I needed to take them back. The docs wouldn't have given them to her if they weren't doing some good. Blah, blah, blah.

Well, let me tell you, I've seen plenty in that place that's not doing anybody a damn shot of good. Making those old ladies lives more miserable than they already are. Ha! Good thing I didn't bring up oxygen machines, eh? When old Ralphie wasn't looking, I tossed those pills into the lake. And that's the last we'll see of them.

So anyway, this is Mrs. Janus. She's gonna go soon too. I just know it.

DIANNE EBERTT BEEAFF has written professionally for many years beginning with magazine journalism. She self-published two books, the best-selling memoir *A Grand Madness, Ten Years on the Road with U2*, and *Homecoming*, a poetry book illustrated with her graphite drawings. More recently she had two other books traditionally published, the award-winning historical fiction novel, *Power's Garden*, and the non-fiction *Spirit Stones, Unraveling the Megalithic Mysteries of Western Europe's Prehistoric Monuments*. She has just recently turned to short fiction. Dianne lives in Tucson, Arizona with her husband Dan. Find her work and writer's blog at www.debeeaff.wordpress.com and on Facebook at Dianne Ebertt Beeaff.

BILL BROWN is the author of ten poetry collections and a textbook. His new collection, *Elemental* (3: A Taos Press) was released in November, 2014. His new chapbook, *Morning Window* (Iris Press) was released January, 2017. The recipient of many fellowships, Brown was awarded the Writer of the Year 2011 by the Tennessee Writers Alliance. His work appears in *Appalachian Heritage, Appalachian Journal, Asheville Poetry Review, Atlanta Review, River Styx, Southern Humanities Review, POEM, Potomac Review, Prairie Schooner, North American Review, Southern Poetry Review, Tar River Review*, and *Cloudbank*, among others.

CHARLOTTE COVEY is from St. Mary's County, Maryland. Currently, she is an MFA candidate in Poetry at the University of Missouri—St. Louis. She has poetry published or forthcoming in *The Normal School, Salamander Review, CALYX Journal, The Minnesota Review,* and *Sonora Review,* among others. In 2017, she was nominated for a Pushcart Prize. She is co-editor-in-chief of *Milk Journal* and an assistant editor for *Natural Bridge.*

MARY CRAWFORD has published stories in several literary journals, including *Salamander, Green Mountains Review,* and *Ghost Parachute.*

ASHLEY FARMER is the author of *The Women* (Civil Coping Mechanisms, 2016), *The Farmacist* (Jellyfish Highway Press, 2015), *Beside Myself* (PANK/Tiny Hardcore Press, 2014), and the chapbook *Farm Town* (Rust Belt Bindery, 2012). A former editor for publications like *Atomica Magazine, Salt Hill Journal,* and others, she currently serves as an editor for *Juked.* She lives in Salt Lake City, UT with her husband, the writer Ryan Ridge.

PETER D. GORMAN is an occasional optimist living in Kensington, MD. His fiction has appeared in *Fugue, Hayden's Ferry Review, The Pinch,* and *Worcester Review,* among others.

JAN C. GROSSMAN's poems have appeared or are forthcoming in *Salmagundi, Tampa Review, Atlanta Review, Poetry East, Plainsongs, Poet Lore, American Arts Quarterly,* and *Potomac Review,* among other journals. She is the recipient of a 2017 *Plainsongs* award. She lives in New York City.

171

Michael Homolka is the author of *Antiquity*, winner of the 2015 Kathryn A. Morton Prize in Poetry from Sarabande Books. His poems have appeared in publications such as *The New Yorker, Ploughshares, The Threepenny Review, Antioch Review, AGNI,* and *Poetry Daily*. A graduate of Bennington College's MFA program, he currently teaches high school students in New York City.

Nancy Keating's poetry has been published in several anthologies and literary magazines, including *New Letters, The Southampton Review, Tar River Poetry, Crab Creek Review, Iconoclast, Chaffin Review,* and *Long Island Quarterly*. She is the author of a collection, *Always Looking Back,* and is pursuing an MFA in creative writing at Stony Brook University.

Harris Lahti is an MFA candidate at Sarah Lawrence College, and an associate editor at *Juked*. His work has appeared in or is forthcoming for *Yemassee, Fanzine, Midwestern Gothic, Potomac Review,* and elsewhere.

Laura Levenson is a writer and psychotherapist in practice in Bangor, Maine for almost 40 years. Her work has appeared in *The Maine Review, Summer Stories* (ShantiArts), and *Maine Voices*.

Lisa A. Levy has a Master of Fine Arts in Fiction from Syracuse University and a Master of Divinity from Yale Divinity School. Her work has appeared in *Opium, The Newtowner, The Perch,* and online at *Killing the Buddha*. She lives in Houston, where she works as a chaplain at a homeless services agency.

Sylvia Liu is an environmental attorney turned author and illustrator. She is the author of the award-winning picture book, *A Morning with Grandpa*, illustrated by Christina Forshay (Lee & Low Books, 2016). She co-runs the kid lit resource website, Kidlit411, named by *Writer's Digest* as one of the 101 Best Websites for Writers for the past three years.

Maya Marshall, an educator, editor, and poet, holds fellowships from Cave Canem and Callaloo. Currently, she serves as a managing editor for *PANK*.

Nancy McCabe is the author of five books, most recently the novel *Following Disasters* and the memoir *From Little Houses to Little Women: Revisiting a Literary Childhood*, due out in paperback this spring. Her work has appeared in *Prairie Schooner, Newsweek, Gulf Coast, Brain Teen*, and *The Los Angeles Review of Books*, among others, received a Pushcart Prize, and been recognized several times on notable lists of Best American anthologies. Her website is nancymccabe.net.

Poet and translator **Karen McPherson** is a professor emerita of French at the University of Oregon. Her book *Skein of Light* (Airlie Press, 2014) was a finalist for the Eric Hoffer Book Award for Poetry. She is also the author of the chapbook *Sketching Elise* and of *Delft Blue & Objects of the World*, a book-length translation into English of poetic essays by Quebec poet Louise Warren. Her work has appeared in numerous literary journals including *Potomac Review, Descant, Cider Press Review,*

Saranac Review, Zoland Poetry Journal, and *Beloit Poetry Journal.* Her website is kmcphersonpoet.com.

TRAVIS MOSSOTTI'S latest collection, *Narcissus Americana,* (University of Arkansas Press, 2018), was selected as the winner of the 2018 Miller Williams Poetry Prize. Mossotti teaches at Webster University and works for Washington University in the Office of the Vice Chancellor for Research.

RAYNALD PATRICE DESMEULES NAYLER'S poetry has been published in the *Beloit Poetry Journal, Weave, Juked, Able Muse, Sentence, Badlands, The Mud Season Review,* and many other magazines both online and in print. Born in the Saguenay-Lac Saint Jean region of Quebec and raised in Northern California, Raynald holds a Masters in Global Diplomacy from SOAS, the University of London, and is a Foreign Service Officer with the Department of State. He served as a Peace Corps Volunteer in Turkmenistan. He is a Russian speaker, and has lived and worked in the countries of Central Asia and the former Soviet Union for over a decade. He currently lives in Baku, Azerbaijan.

JOHN A. NIEVES'S poems appear in journals such as *Beloit Poetry Journal, Mid-American Review, Puerto del Sol, American Literary Review,* and *Poetry Northwest.* He won the *Indiana Review* Poetry Prize. His first book, *Curio,* won the Elixir Press Annual Judges Prize, and came out in 2014. He is Assistant Professor of English at Salisbury University.

DOUGLAS NORDFORS is a native of Seattle, who lives in Charlottesville, Virginia. Since 1987, he has published poems in such journals as *Poet Lore*, *Quarterly West*, *The Iowa Review*, and *Poetry Northwest*. His most recent work has appeared or is forthcoming in *The Louisville Review*, *The Comstock Review*, *Matter*, *The Tulane Review*, and others. He has published two books of poetry, *Auras* (2008) and *The Fate Motif* (2013).

JARED PEARCE'S poems have recently been or will soon be shared in *Red Fez*, *The Lampeter Review*, *Red River Review*, *Review Americana*, and *Rosebud*. His debut collection from Aubade Press is due next year. He lives in Iowa.

ROBERT RICE'S stories and poems have appeared or are forthcoming in various literary magazines, including *Hayden's Ferry Review*, *New Letters*, *The North American Review*, *The Saint Ann's Review*, and *West Wind Review*. He has also published four novels, including *The Last Pendragon* and *The Nature of Midnight*, and a memoir of six months spent alone in the Montana wilderness, *Walking into Silence*.

ROBIN RICHSTONE is a poet, painter, and gardener who moved to Michigan from California a few years ago and is still adjusting. Her poems have been published in *Poetry*, *Borderlands*, *New England Review*, *North American Review*, and other magazines, many under her former name of Robin Shectman. Her website is robinrichstone.wordpress.com.

Esteban Rodríguez holds an MFA from the University of Texas Pan-American. His poetry has appeared or is forthcoming in *The Gettysburg Review*, *Notre Dame Review*, *Hayden's Ferry Review*, *New England Review*, *Puerto del Sol*, and *The Carolina Quarterly*. He lives in Austin, Texas.

Ben Rosenthal is a writer living in New York. He has had residencies at The MacDowell Colony and at Ucross, and will graduate from Columbia University this February with an MFA in Fiction.

Anna Saikin's stories have appeared in *Pretty Owl Poetry*, *Halo*, *Per Contra*, *Gravel*, and elsewhere. She teaches music and writing, and can be found on Twitter @AnnaSaikin.

G.J. Sanford is an MFA candidate in Poetry at the University of Nevada—Reno. Their work has appeared or is forthcoming in *Rust + Moth*, *River Styx Magazine*, *After the Pause*, and *Clover: A Literary Rag*. They currently reside in a tiny house with their tiny cat muse, Finn.

Amy Sawyer is a poet residing in Washington, DC. She studied philosophy and religion at Clemson University and earned her MFA at Converse College. Her work has been published in numerous journals such as *Stand Magazine*, *Mud Season Review*, *Mom Egg Review*, *Pembroke Magazine*, *Louisiana Literature*, and *South Carolina Review*. She reads for *Ruminate Magazine* and was previously the Review Editor for *South 85 Journal*.

MARJORIE STELMACH is the author of five volumes of poems, most recently *Falter* (Cascade Books, 2017). Her work has appeared in *Boulevard, Florida Review, Gettysburg Review, Hudson Review, Image, New Letters,* and *Tampa Review.* She is the recipient of the 2016 Chad Walsh Poetry Prize from *The Beloit Poetry Journal.*

ASHLEY STIMPSON is a freelance writer based in Baltimore. She writes memoirs for other people and poetry for herself.

MARIA TERRONE'S nonfiction has appeared in such journals as *Witness, Green Mountains Review, The Common,* and Bordighera Press will publish her debut book of personal essays, *At Home in the New World,* later this year. A Pushcart-nominated poet whose work has been published in French and Farsi, she is the author of the collections *Eye to Eye, A Secret Room in Fall* (McGovern Prize, Ashland Poetry Press), *The Bodies We Were Loaned,* and a chapbook, *American Gothic, Take 2.* In 2015 she became the poetry editor of the journal *Italian Americana.* www.mariaterrone.com

AMY TROTTER is an Alabama native living near DC, where she is working towards her MFA in Poetry at American University. She is also a photographer and poetry editor for *District Lit.* Her work has appeared in *Mezzo Cammin* and the *American Journal of Poetry.*

P. IVAN YOUNG is author of *Smell of Salt, Ghost of Rain* (Brick House Books, 2015) and the chapbook, *A Shape in the Waves* (Stepping Stones Press, 2008). He received an Individual Artist Award from the Maryland State Arts

Council (2011), and is the 2013 winner of the Norton Girault Literary Prize. His most recent publications are in *American Life in Poetry, Apple Valley Review, The Baltimore Review, The Louisville Review, Cider Press Review, Watershed Review, Passages North, The Southeast Review,* and *Hayden's Ferry Review.* He is currently a doctoral student in English at University of Nebraska Lincoln, where he reads for Prairie Schooner.

www.ingramcontent.com/pod-product-compliance
Lightning Source LLC
Chambersburg PA
CBHW032008170626
46807CB00006B/2707